D1164586

SONG OF ROBIN HOOD

SELECTED & EDITED
BY ANNE MALCOLMSON

MUSIC ARRANGED BY
GRACE CASTAGNETTA

DESIGNED & ILLUSTRATED
BY VIRGINIA LEE BURTON

PUBLISHED BY HOUGHTON MIFFLIN CO.

1947

3 1901 02882 8798

Copyright © 1947 by Anne Burnett Malcolmson and Virginia Lee Demetrios
Copyright © renewed 1975 by Grace Castagnetta, Aristides Burton Demetrios and Michael Burton Demetrios

All rights reserved. For information about permission
to reproduce selections from this book, write to
Permissions, Houghton Mifflin Company,
215 Park Avenue South, New York, New York 10003.

www.hmco.com/trade

Library of Congress Cataloging-in-Publication Number
00-132463

ISBN 0-618-07186-5

Manufactured in the United States of America
CRW 10 9 8 7 6 5 4 3 2 1

For Charles Malcolmson

PREFACE

Unfortunately, in presenting folklore to the public, many editors have tried to interpret it unnecessarily and have often distorted it in the process. Consequently the lore we offer is not folklore in the truest sense; our well-meant services are sometimes disservices, both to the reader and to his traditional heritage.

There are, of course, sound reasons for editing and retelling old material. The ordinary individual can hardly be expected to read *Beowulf* in the original. He is limited technically by his lack of knowledge of languages. But when we simplify or translate with the reader's limitations in mind, we must remember also the spirit and intention of the original story-teller. Wherever possible the past should be allowed to speak for itself.

Robin Hood has suffered as much as any hero from his interpreters. The canny yeoman of Sherwood Forest has become a romantic aristocrat given to the athletic courtship of distressed beauty, a shining light of feudalism and of chivalry in the medieval sense.

In none of the earliest ballads about him, those known to have been sung in the thirteenth and fourteenth centuries, does he appear as a nobleman. His popularity in those days rested upon the fact that he represented the emerging middle class, which created him. Not until ballad-making became a literary fad of the eighteenth century did he become the Earl of Huntington.

If Robin's story had been told originally in involved, difficult form or in an obscure tongue, there might be some reason for all the interpreting. However, most of the old songs about him are simple, in a language very close to our own. With few minor changes, most of these in spelling, they can be read easily and pleasurably by most people today. It's a pity that they have lain so long neglected by all except scholars and antiquarians. Therefore this book.

Some editing has been necessary. In places the Early Modern English of the songs is more Early than Modern. Words and idioms current in the fourteenth century have long since passed into limbo.

Many of the ballads were originally very long. These have been cut wherever possible without hurting the story. Similarly a number of the ballads which belong properly to the Robin Hood cycle have been omitted. Some have been dropped because only fragments of the texts remain, others because they are essentially repetitions of those included here, and still others simply for lack of space.

Many ballad anthologists have succumbed to an unfortunate habit of dis-

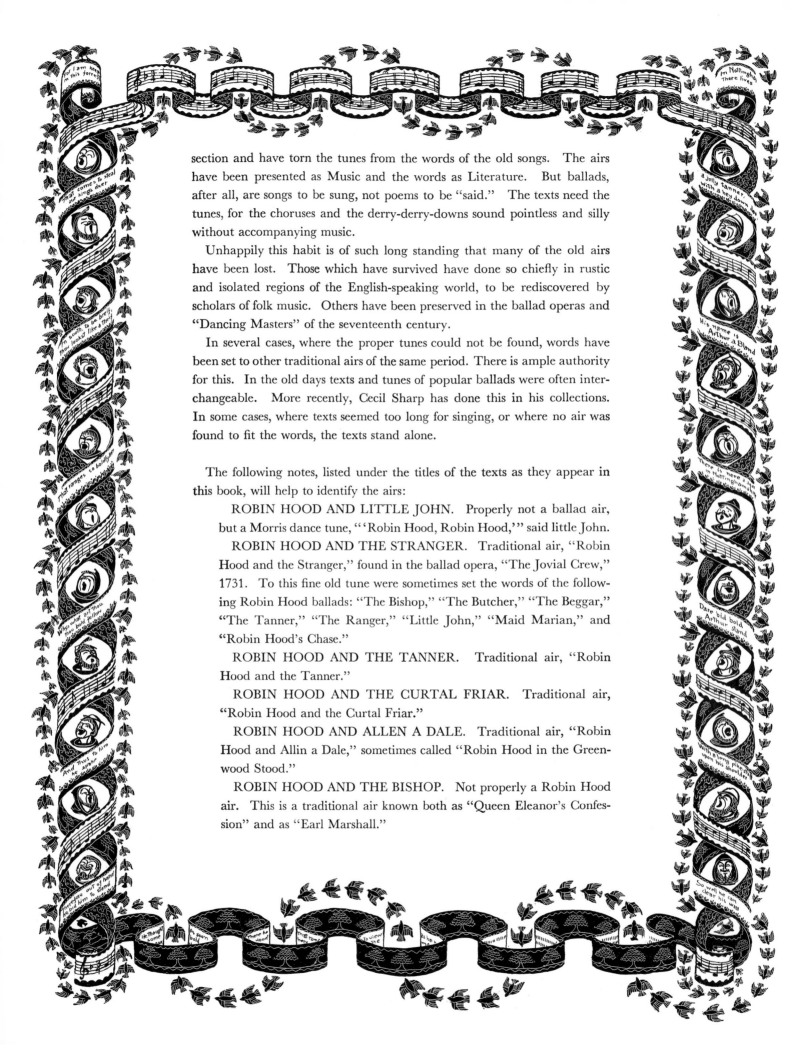

section and have torn the tunes from the words of the old songs. The airs have been presented as Music and the words as Literature. But ballads, after all, are songs to be sung, not poems to be "said." The texts need the tunes, for the choruses and the derry-derry-downs sound pointless and silly without accompanying music.

Unhappily this habit is of such long standing that many of the old airs have been lost. Those which have survived have done so chiefly in rustic and isolated regions of the English-speaking world, to be rediscovered by scholars of folk music. Others have been preserved in the ballad operas and "Dancing Masters" of the seventeenth century.

In several cases, where the proper tunes could not be found, words have been set to other traditional airs of the same period. There is ample authority for this. In the old days texts and tunes of popular ballads were often interchangeable. More recently, Cecil Sharp has done this in his collections. In some cases, where texts seemed too long for singing, or where no air was found to fit the words, the texts stand alone.

The following notes, listed under the titles of the texts as they appear in this book, will help to identify the airs:

ROBIN HOOD AND LITTLE JOHN. Properly not a ballad air, but a Morris dance tune, "'Robin Hood, Robin Hood,'" said little John.

ROBIN HOOD AND THE STRANGER. Traditional air, "Robin Hood and the Stranger," found in the ballad opera, "The Jovial Crew," 1731. To this fine old tune were sometimes set the words of the following Robin Hood ballads: "The Bishop," "The Butcher," "The Beggar," "The Tanner," "The Ranger," "Little John," "Maid Marian," and "Robin Hood's Chase."

ROBIN HOOD AND THE TANNER. Traditional air, "Robin Hood and the Tanner."

ROBIN HOOD AND THE CURTAL FRIAR. Traditional air, "Robin Hood and the Curtal Friar."

ROBIN HOOD AND ALLEN A DALE. Traditional air, "Robin Hood and Allin a Dale," sometimes called "Robin Hood in the Greenwood Stood."

ROBIN HOOD AND THE BISHOP. Not properly a Robin Hood air. This is a traditional air known both as "Queen Eleanor's Confession" and as "Earl Marshall."

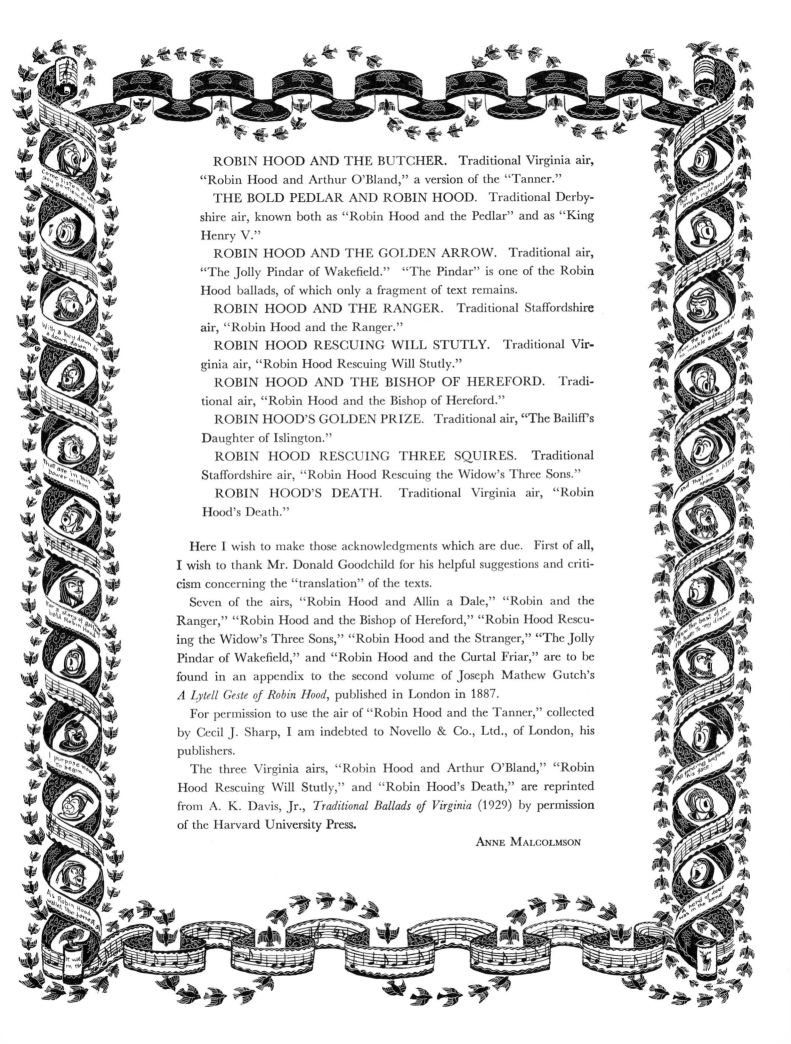

ROBIN HOOD AND THE BUTCHER. Traditional Virginia air, "Robin Hood and Arthur O'Bland," a version of the "Tanner."

THE BOLD PEDLAR AND ROBIN HOOD. Traditional Derbyshire air, known both as "Robin Hood and the Pedlar" and as "King Henry V."

ROBIN HOOD AND THE GOLDEN ARROW. Traditional air, "The Jolly Pindar of Wakefield." "The Pindar" is one of the Robin Hood ballads, of which only a fragment of text remains.

ROBIN HOOD AND THE RANGER. Traditional Staffordshire air, "Robin Hood and the Ranger."

ROBIN HOOD RESCUING WILL STUTLY. Traditional Virginia air, "Robin Hood Rescuing Will Stutly."

ROBIN HOOD AND THE BISHOP OF HEREFORD. Traditional air, "Robin Hood and the Bishop of Hereford."

ROBIN HOOD'S GOLDEN PRIZE. Traditional air, "The Bailiff's Daughter of Islington."

ROBIN HOOD RESCUING THREE SQUIRES. Traditional Staffordshire air, "Robin Hood Rescuing the Widow's Three Sons."

ROBIN HOOD'S DEATH. Traditional Virginia air, "Robin Hood's Death."

Here I wish to make those acknowledgments which are due. First of all, I wish to thank Mr. Donald Goodchild for his helpful suggestions and criticism concerning the "translation" of the texts.

Seven of the airs, "Robin Hood and Allin a Dale," "Robin and the Ranger," "Robin Hood and the Bishop of Hereford," "Robin Hood Rescuing the Widow's Three Sons," "Robin Hood and the Stranger," "The Jolly Pindar of Wakefield," and "Robin Hood and the Curtal Friar," are to be found in an appendix to the second volume of Joseph Mathew Gutch's *A Lytell Geste of Robin Hood*, published in London in 1887.

For permission to use the air of "Robin Hood and the Tanner," collected by Cecil J. Sharp, I am indebted to Novello & Co., Ltd., of London, his publishers.

The three Virginia airs, "Robin Hood and Arthur O'Bland," "Robin Hood Rescuing Will Stutly," and "Robin Hood's Death," are reprinted from A. K. Davis, Jr., *Traditional Ballads of Virginia* (1929) by permission of the Harvard University Press.

ANNE MALCOLMSON

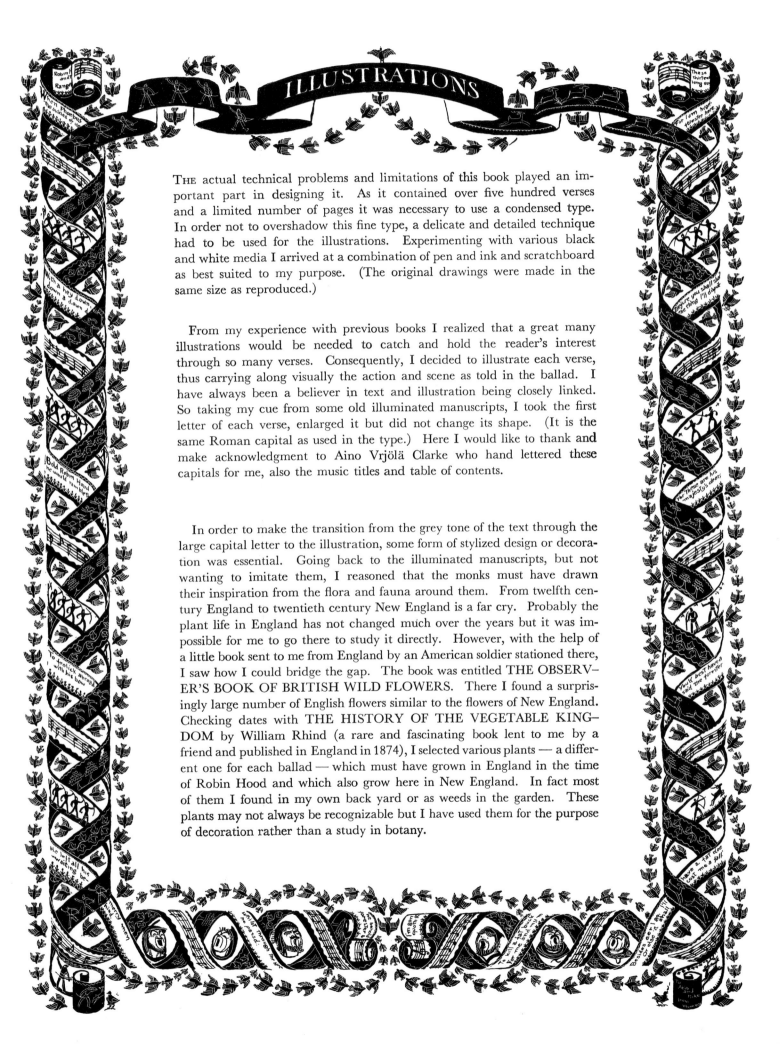

ILLUSTRATIONS

THE actual technical problems and limitations of this book played an important part in designing it. As it contained over five hundred verses and a limited number of pages it was necessary to use a condensed type. In order not to overshadow this fine type, a delicate and detailed technique had to be used for the illustrations. Experimenting with various black and white media I arrived at a combination of pen and ink and scratchboard as best suited to my purpose. (The original drawings were made in the same size as reproduced.)

From my experience with previous books I realized that a great many illustrations would be needed to catch and hold the reader's interest through so many verses. Consequently, I decided to illustrate each verse, thus carrying along visually the action and scene as told in the ballad. I have always been a believer in text and illustration being closely linked. So taking my cue from some old illuminated manuscripts, I took the first letter of each verse, enlarged it but did not change its shape. (It is the same Roman capital as used in the type.) Here I would like to thank and make acknowledgment to Aino Vrjölä Clarke who hand lettered these capitals for me, also the music titles and table of contents.

In order to make the transition from the grey tone of the text through the large capital letter to the illustration, some form of stylized design or decoration was essential. Going back to the illuminated manuscripts, but not wanting to imitate them, I reasoned that the monks must have drawn their inspiration from the flora and fauna around them. From twelfth century England to twentieth century New England is a far cry. Probably the plant life in England has not changed much over the years but it was impossible for me to go there to study it directly. However, with the help of a little book sent to me from England by an American soldier stationed there, I saw how I could bridge the gap. The book was entitled THE OBSERV-ER'S BOOK OF BRITISH WILD FLOWERS. There I found a surprisingly large number of English flowers similar to the flowers of New England. Checking dates with THE HISTORY OF THE VEGETABLE KING-DOM by William Rhind (a rare and fascinating book lent to me by a friend and published in England in 1874), I selected various plants — a different one for each ballad — which must have grown in England in the time of Robin Hood and which also grow here in New England. In fact most of them I found in my own back yard or as weeds in the garden. These plants may not always be recognizable but I have used them for the purpose of decoration rather than a study in botany.

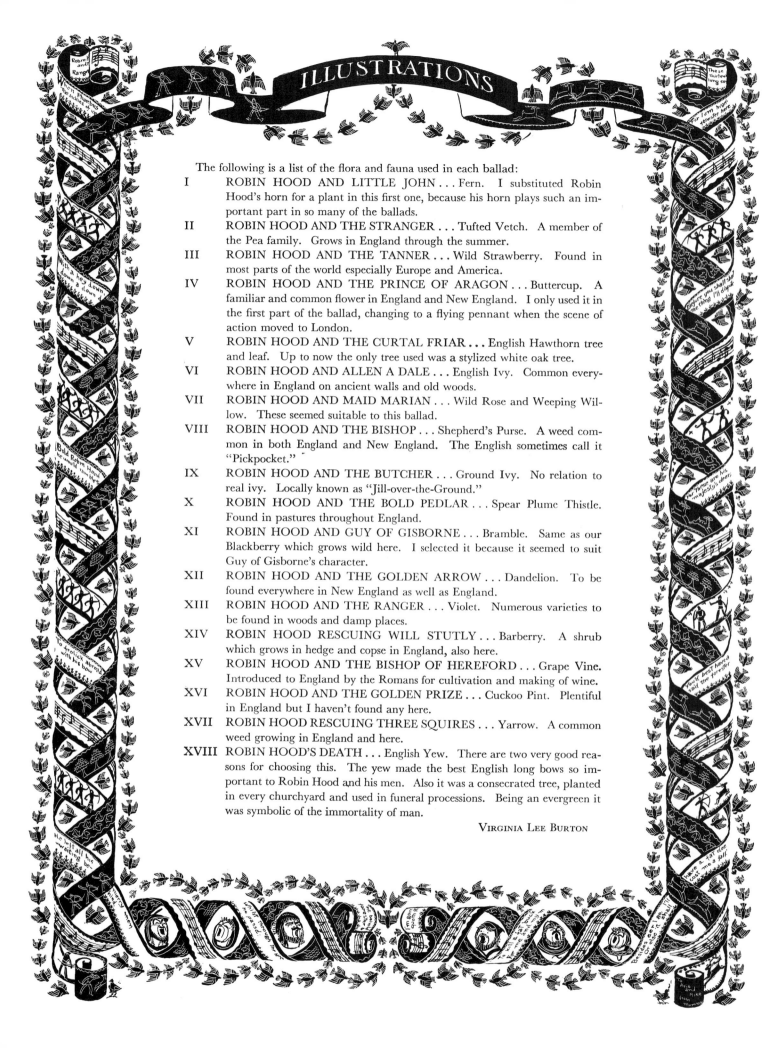

ILLUSTRATIONS

The following is a list of the flora and fauna used in each ballad:

I ROBIN HOOD AND LITTLE JOHN ... Fern. I substituted Robin Hood's horn for a plant in this first one, because his horn plays such an important part in so many of the ballads.

II ROBIN HOOD AND THE STRANGER ... Tufted Vetch. A member of the Pea family. Grows in England through the summer.

III ROBIN HOOD AND THE TANNER ... Wild Strawberry. Found in most parts of the world especially Europe and America.

IV ROBIN HOOD AND THE PRINCE OF ARAGON ... Buttercup. A familiar and common flower in England and New England. I only used it in the first part of the ballad, changing to a flying pennant when the scene of action moved to London.

V ROBIN HOOD AND THE CURTAL FRIAR ... English Hawthorn tree and leaf. Up to now the only tree used was a stylized white oak tree.

VI ROBIN HOOD AND ALLEN A DALE ... English Ivy. Common everywhere in England on ancient walls and old woods.

VII ROBIN HOOD AND MAID MARIAN ... Wild Rose and Weeping Willow. These seemed suitable to this ballad.

VIII ROBIN HOOD AND THE BISHOP ... Shepherd's Purse. A weed common in both England and New England. The English sometimes call it "Pickpocket."

IX ROBIN HOOD AND THE BUTCHER ... Ground Ivy. No relation to real ivy. Locally known as "Jill-over-the-Ground."

X ROBIN HOOD AND THE BOLD PEDLAR ... Spear Plume Thistle. Found in pastures throughout England.

XI ROBIN HOOD AND GUY OF GISBORNE ... Bramble. Same as our Blackberry which grows wild here. I selected it because it seemed to suit Guy of Gisborne's character.

XII ROBIN HOOD AND THE GOLDEN ARROW ... Dandelion. To be found everywhere in New England as well as England.

XIII ROBIN HOOD AND THE RANGER ... Violet. Numerous varieties to be found in woods and damp places.

XIV ROBIN HOOD RESCUING WILL STUTLY ... Barberry. A shrub which grows in hedge and copse in England, also here.

XV ROBIN HOOD AND THE BISHOP OF HEREFORD ... Grape Vine. Introduced to England by the Romans for cultivation and making of wine.

XVI ROBIN HOOD AND THE GOLDEN PRIZE ... Cuckoo Pint. Plentiful in England but I haven't found any here.

XVII ROBIN HOOD RESCUING THREE SQUIRES ... Yarrow. A common weed growing in England and here.

XVIII ROBIN HOOD'S DEATH ... English Yew. There are two very good reasons for choosing this. The yew made the best English long bows so important to Robin Hood and his men. Also it was a consecrated tree, planted in every churchyard and used in funeral processions. Being an evergreen it was symbolic of the immortality of man.

VIRGINIA LEE BURTON

TABLE OF CONTENTS

ROBIN HOOD AND LITTLE JOHN

With spirit and marked rhythm

1. When Rob - in Hood was a - bout twen - ty years old, He hap - pened to meet Lit - tle John, O. A jol - ly brisk blade, ___ right fit for the trade, ___ For
2. Though he was called Lit - tle, his limbs they were large; His sta - ture was sev - en feet high, O. Wher - ev - er he came, ___ they quaked at his name, ___ For
3. Bold Rob - in Hood said to his jol - ly bow - men, "Pray, tar - ry you here in this grove, O. And see that you all ___ ob - serve well my call ___ While

10

he	was	a	lus	— ty	young		man,		O.	
soon	he	would	make	them	all		fly,		O.	
through __	the	for	— est	I		rove,		O."		

We have had no sport for these fourteen long days;
Therefore now abroad will I go.
Now should I be beat and cannot retreat
My horn I will presently blow."

Robin shook hands with his merry men all,
And bade them at present good-bye.
Then as near a brook his journey he took
A stranger he chanced to espy.

They happened to meet on a long narrow bridge,
And neither of them would give way.
Quoth bold Robin Hood, and sturdily stood,
"I'll show you some Nottingham play."

With that from his quiver an arrow he drew,
A broad arrow with a goose-wing.
The stranger replied, "I'll licker thy hide
If thou offer to touch but the string."

Quoth bold Robin Hood, "Thou dost prate like an ass;
For were I to bend but my bow,
I could send a dart quite through thy proud heart
Before thou could strike me one blow."

Thou talkst like a coward," the stranger replied,
"Well armed with a long-bow you stand
To shoot at my breast; while I, I protest,
Have naught but a staff in my hand."

"The name of a coward," quoth Robin, "I scorn.
　Therefore my long-bow I'll lay by.
And now for thy sake a staff I will take,
　Thy courage and manhood to try."

Then Robin Hood stepped to a thicket of trees,
　And chose him a staff of ground-oak.
Now this being done, away he did run
　To the stranger, and merrily spoke:

Lo! See my staff! It is lusty and tough.
　Now here on the bridge we will play.
Whoever falls in, the other shall win
　The battle and so we'll away."

With all my whole heart," the stranger replied,
　"I scorn in the least to give out."
This said, they fell to it without more dispute,
　And their staffs they did flourish about.

First Robin Hood gave the stranger a bang,
　So hard that it made his bones ring.
The stranger he said, "This must be repaid.
　I'll give you as good as you bring."

The stranger gave Robin a crack on the crown,
　Which caused the blood to appear.
Then Robin, enraged, more fiercely engaged,
　And followed his blows more severe.

So, then into fury the stranger he flew,
　And gave him a terrible look,
And with it a blow that laid him full low
　And tumbled him into the brook.

"I prithee, good fellow, O, where art thou now?"
　The stranger, in laughter, he cried.
Quoth bold Robin Hood, "Good faith, in the flood,
　And floating along with the tide.

I needs must acknowledge thou art a brave soul;
　With thee I'll no longer contend.
For needs must I say, thou hast won the day.
　Our battle shall be at an end."

12

Then unto the bank he did presently wade
  And pulled himself out by a thorn;
Which done, at the last, he blew a loud blast
  Straightway on his fine bugle-horn.

The echo of this through the valleys did fly,
  At which his stout bowmen appeared,
All clothed in green, most gay to be seen,
  And up to their master they steered.

"O, what is the matter?" Will Stutly said,
  "Good master, you're wet to the skin."
"No matter," quoth he, "the lad which you see
  In fighting hath tumbled me in."

"He'll not go scot free," the others replied;
  So straight they were seizing him there
To duck him likewise. But Robin Hood cries,
  "He is a stout fellow. Forbear!

"There's no one shall wrong thee, friend. Be not afraid.
  These bowmen upon me do wait.
There's three score and nine. If thou wilt be mine,
  Thou shalt have a livery straight,

"And other fine trappings so fit for a man.
  Speak up, jolly blade, never fear.
I'll teach you also the use of the bow
  To shoot at the fat fallow-deer."

"O, here is my hand," the stranger replied,
  "I'll serve you with all my whole heart.
My name is John Little, a man of good mettle;
  Ne'er doubt me, for I'll play my part."

"His name shall be changed," quoth Will Stutly then,
  "And I will his godfather be.
Prepare then a feast, and none of the least,
  For we will be merry," quoth he.

They presently fetched in a pair of fat does,
  With humming strong liquor likewise.
They loved what was good. So in the greenwood
  This pretty sweet babe they baptize.

13

He was, I must tell you, but seven feet high,
　　And maybe an ell in the waist,
A pretty sweet lad. Much feasting they had.
　　Bold Robin the christening graced.

Quoth Stutly, "This infant John Little was called,
　　Which name shall be changéd anon.
The words we'll transpose; so, wherever he goes,
　　His name shall be called Little John."

Then Robin he took the pretty sweet babe
　　And clothed him from top to the toe
In garments of green, most gay to be seen,
　　And gave him a curious long-bow.

Thou shalt be an archer as well as the best,
　　And range in the greenwood with us;
Where we'll not want gold nor silver, behold,
　　While bishops have ought in their purse."

And so ever after, as long as he lived,
　　Although he was proper and tall,
Yet, nevertheless, the truth to express,
　　Still Little John they did him call.

ROBIN HOOD AND THE STRANGER

Lively

1. Come, lis-ten a while you
2. As Rob-in Hood walked a
3. His doub-let was of

gen-tle-men all,
long the wood,
silk, he said,

With a hey down, down a down down,

That
It
His

CHORUS

are in this bow-er with-in;
was in the heat of the day,
stock-ings like scar-let shone.

For a sto-ry of gal-lant
There did he meet as
And he walked on a

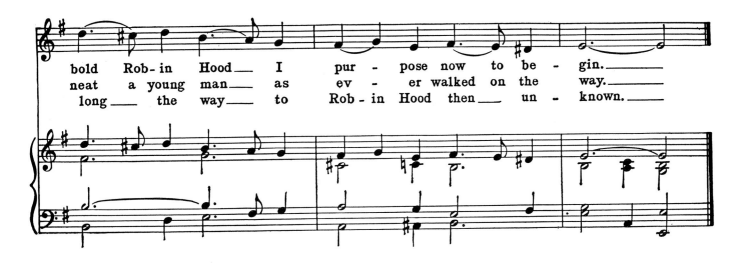

bold Rob-in Hood ___ I pur - pose now to be - gin. ___
neat a young man ___ as ev - er walked on the way. ___
long ___ the way ___ to Rob-in Hood then ___ un - known. ___

A herd of deer was in the bend,
   Grazing before him there.
"The best of ye I'll have for my dinner,
   And that with a right good cheer."

The stranger made but little ado;
   He bent a right good bow.
The very best buck in the herd he slew
   Forty good yards him fro.

"Well shot, well shot!" quoth Robin Hood then,
   "That shot it was shot in time.
And if thou wilt accept the place
   Thou shalt be a bold yeoman of mine."

"Go play the coward," the stranger said,
   "Make haste, and quickly give o'er.
Or with my fist, be sure of this,
   I'll give thee of blows a score."

"Thou hadst best not buffet me," Robin said,
   "For though I seem forlorn,
Yet I have those who take my part
   If I but blow my horn."

"Thou hadst best not blow it," the stranger said,
   "Be thou never so much in haste;
For I can draw out a good broad sword
   And quickly cut the blast."

17

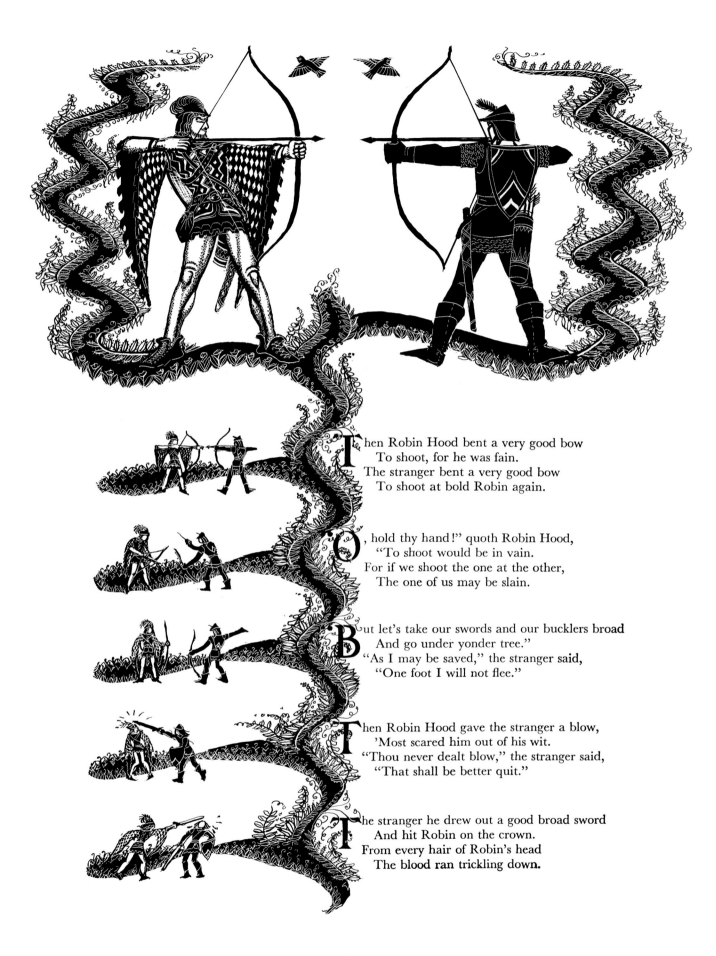

Then Robin Hood bent a very good bow
  To shoot, for he was fain.
The stranger bent a very good bow
  To shoot at bold Robin again.

O, hold thy hand!" quoth Robin Hood,
  "To shoot would be in vain.
For if we shoot the one at the other,
  The one of us may be slain.

But let's take our swords and our bucklers broad
  And go under yonder tree."
"As I may be saved," the stranger said,
  "One foot I will not flee."

Then Robin Hood gave the stranger a blow,
  'Most scared him out of his wit.
"Thou never dealt blow," the stranger said,
  "That shall be better quit."

The stranger he drew out a good broad sword
  And hit Robin on the crown.
From every hair of Robin's head
  The blood ran trickling down.

"Have mercy, good fellow," quoth Robin Hood then,
    "This blow hath struck me well.
Tell me, good fellow, who thou art,
    Tell me where thou dost dwell."

The stranger answered bold Robin Hood then,
    "I'll tell thee where I did dwell.
In Maxfield was I bred and born;
    My name is young Gamwell.

"For killing my father's steward," he said,
    "I'm forced to this English wood,
And for to seek an uncle of mine.
    Some call him Robin Hood."

"But art thou a cousin of Robin Hood's, then?
    The sooner we should have done."
"As I may be saved," the stranger said,
    "I am his own sister's son."

But, O! What kissing and courting was there
    When these two cousins did greet!
Together they walked all that summer's day
    And with Little John did meet.

19

But when they met with Little John,
　To Robin he there did say,
"O, master, master, where have you been,
　And tarried so long away?"

"**I** met with a stranger," quoth Robin Hood then,
　"Full sore he hath beaten me."
"Then I'll have a bout with him," said John,
　"And see if he can beat me."

"**O**h no! Oh no!" quoth Robin Hood then,
　"Little John, it may not be.
For he's my own dear sister's son
　And cousin unto me.

But he shall be a bold yeoman of mine,
　My chief man next to thee.
And I Robin Hood, and thou Little John,
　And Scarlet he shall be.

And we'll be three of the bravest outlaws
　That are in the North Countree."
If you will have more of bold Robin Hood
　In other tales it shall be.

20

ROBIN HOOD AND THE TANNER

With lilting rhythm

1. In Not - ting - ham there lived a jol - ly tan - ner; His
2. __ With a long staff up - on __ his shoul - der, So
3. As Ar - thur went forth one sum - mer's morn - ing to the

name __ was Ar - thur a Bland. There was ne - 'er a
well he could clear __ his way; By __ two and by
for - est of mer - ry Sher - wood, To __ view the red

squire __ in Not - ting - ham - shire Dared bid __ bold
three __ he made them to flee, For he had no
deer __ that range here and there, There met he with

22

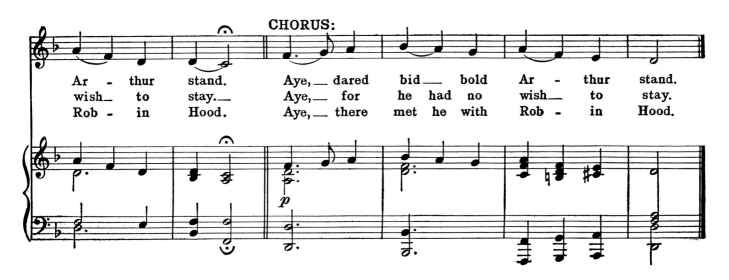

CHORUS:

Ar - thur stand.   Aye, __ dared bid __ bold Ar - thur stand.
wish __ to stay. __   Aye, __ for he had no wish __ to stay.
Rob - in Hood.   Aye, __ there met he with Rob - in Hood.

As soon as bold Robin did him espy,
  He thought some sport he would make;
Therefore out of hand he bade him to stand,
  And thus to him he spake:

Why, what art thou, thou bold fellow,
  That ranges so boldly here?
In sooth, to be brief, thou lookst like a thief,
  That comes to steal our King's deer.

For I am a keeper in this wood;
  The King puts me here in trust
To look to his deer that range here and there.
  Stay thee therefore I must."

If thou be a keeper in this wood
  And have such a great command,
Yet thou must have more of thy fellows in store
  Before thou make me to stand."

Nay, I have no more of my fellows in store,
  Or any that I do need.
But I have a staff of another oak graff;
  I know it will do the deed."

For thy sword and thy bow I care not a straw,
  Nor for all thine arrows to boot.
If I get a knop upon thy bare scop
  Thou canst as well shout as shoot."

"Speak cleanly, good fellow," said Robin Hood,
"And give better terms to me.
Else I'll thee correct for thy neglect
And make thee more mannerly."

Then Robin Hood he unbuckled his belt;
He laid down his bow so long;
He took up a staff of another oak graff
That was both stout and strong.

"I'll yield to thy weapon," said Robin Hood,
"Since thou wilt not yield to mine;
For I have a staff of another oak graff,
Not half a foot longer than thine.

"But let me measure," said Robin Hood,
"Before we begin our fray.
I'll not have mine to be longer than thine,
For that would be called foul play."

"I care not for its length," bold Arthur replied,
"My staff is of oak so free.
Eight feet and a half, it will knock down a calf,
And I hope it will knock down thee."

Then Robin Hood could no longer forbear;
He gave Arthur such a knock
That quickly and soon the blood came down
Before it was ten o'clock.

Then Arthur he soon recovered himself,
And gave him a knock on the crown.
On every hair of bold Robin's head
The blood came trickling down.

Then Robin Hood ragéd like a wild boar,
As soon as he saw his own blood.
And Bland was in haste, he laid on so fast
As though he'd been staking of wood.

And knock for knock they sturdily dealt,
Which held for two hours and more;
So that all the woods rang at every bang,
They plied their work so sore.

"O, hold thy hand," said Robin Hood,
"And let our quarrel fall.
For here we may thresh our bones into mesh,
And get no coin at all.

"What tradesman art thou?" said jolly Robin,
"Good fellow, I prithee me show;
And also me tell in what place thou dost dwell,
For both these fain would I know."

"I am a tanner," bold Arthur replied,
"In Nottingham long have I wrought.
And if thou'lt come there, I vow and I swear
I'll tan thy hide for naught."

"Thank you, good fellow," said jolly Robin,
"Since thou art so kind to me.
And if thou wilt tan my hide for naught,
I will do as much for thee.

"But if thou'lt forsake thy tanner's trade
And live in the greenwood with me, —
My name's Robin Hood, — I swear by the Rood
I'll give thee both gold and fee."

"If thou'rt Robin Hood," bold Arthur replied,
"As I think well thou art,
Then here's my hand; my name's Arthur a Bland;
We two will never depart.

"But tell me, O, tell me, where's Little John?
Of him fain would I hear.
For we are allied by the mothers' side,
And he is my kinsman near."

Then Robin Hood blew on his bugle-horn,
He blew both loud and shrill.
And quickly anon appeared Little John,
Tripping down a green hill.

"O, what is the matter?" said Little John,
"Master, I pray you tell.
Why do you stand with your staff in your hand?
I fear all is not well."

Oman, I do stand, he makes me to stand,
The tanner that stands thee beside.
He's a bonny blade, master of his trade,
For well he hath tanned my hide."

He's to be commended," then said Little John,
"If such a feat he can do.
If he be so stout, we shall have a bout,
And he shall tan my hide, too."

O, hold thy hand," said Robin Hood then,
"For as I understand
He's a yeoman good of thine own blood,
His name is Arthur a Bland."

Then Robin Hood took them both by the hand,
And danced round about the oak tree.
"For three merry men, and three merry men,
And three merry men we be.

And ever hereafter, as long as we live,
We three shall be all one.
The wood shall ring, and the old wife sing,
Of Robin Hood, Arthur, and John."

Robin Hood, Scarlet, and Little John
  Were walking over the plain
With a good fat buck which Scarlet
  With his strong bow had slain.

They'd not walked long within the wood,
  When Robin was espied
Of a beautiful damsel all alone
  That on a black palfrey did ride.

Her riding suit was of sable black;
  A veil hung over her face
Through which her rose-like cheeks did blush
  All with a comely grace.

"Come, what is the matter, thou pretty one?"
  Quoth Robin, "And tell me aright
Whence thou comest and whither thou goest
  All in this mournful plight."

"From London I come," the damsel said,
  "From London on the Thames.
Surrounded it is, O grief to tell!
  Besieged with foreign arms

By the proud Prince of Aragon.
  He swears by his martial hand
To have the Princess for his wife
  Or else to waste this land;

Save that champions can be found
  Who dare fight three to three
Against the Prince and giants twain,
  Most horrid for to see.

Their grisly looks and eyes like swords
  Strike terror where they come.
They've serpents hissing on their helms
  Instead of feathered plume.

"The Princess shall be the victor's prize,
   The King hath vowed and said.
He that shall the contest win
   Shall have her for his bride.

Now we're four damsels sent abroad
   To the east, west, south, and north,
To see whose fortune is so good
   To bring such champions forth.

But all in vain we've sought them out.
   Still none so bold there are
That dare endanger life and blood
   To free a lady fair."

"When is the day?" quoth Robin Hood,
   "Tell me this and no more."
"Midsummer next," the damsel said,
   "Which is June the twenty-four."

The tears then trickled down her cheeks,
   And silent was her tongue.
With sighs and sobs she took her leave;
   Away her palfrey sprung.

Said Robin, "I'll fight the giants all
   To set the lady free!"
"May the devil take me," quoth Little John,
   "If I part from thy company."

"Must I stay behind?" quoth Will Scarlet,
   "No, no! That must not be.
I'll make the third man in the fight,
   So we shall be three to three."

These words cheered Robin to the heart;
   Joy shone within his face.
Within his arms he hugged them both
   And did them both embrace.

Quoth he, "We'll put on mothly grey,
    With a long staff in our hand,
A scrip and bottle by our side
    As come from the Holy Land.

So we may pass along the way.
    None will ask whence we came,
But take us pilgrims for to be
    Or else some holy men."

Now they are on their journey gone
    As fast as they may speed.
Yet, for all their haste, ere they arrived,
    The Princess forth was led

To be delivered to the Prince,
    Who in the lists did stand
Prepared to fight or else receive
    His lady by the hand.

Proudly he walked about the lists,
    His giants by his side.
"Bring forth," said he, "your champions,
    Or bring me forth my bride.

This is the four-and-twentieth day,
    The day we fixed upon.
Bring forth my bride, — or London burns,
    I swear by Acaron."

Then cried the King and Queen likewise,
    Both weeping as they spake.
"Lo! we have brought our daughter dear,
    Whom we must now forsake."

With that stepped out bold Robin Hood.
 "My liege, 't must not be so.
Such beauty as the fair Princess
 Is not for a tyrant's mow."

The Prince he then began to storm.
 "Fool! Maniac! Baboon!
How dare thou keep me from my prize?
 I'll kill thee with a frown!"

Thou tyrant Turk! Thou infidel!"
 Thus Robin did reply,
"Thy frown I scorn! Lo! Here's my gage!
 And thus I thee defie!

And for these two Goliaths here
 That stand on either side,
Here are two little Davids by
 That soon can tame their pride."

Then did the King for armor send,
 For lances, swords, and shields.
And thus all three in armor bright
 Came marching to the field.

The Prince reached Robin such a blow —
 He struck with might and main —
It made him reel about the field
 As though he had been slain.

Thank you," quoth Robin, "for that blow!
 The quarrel shall soon be tried.
This stroke shall strike a full divorce
 Between thee and thy bride."

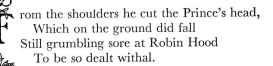

From the shoulders he cut the Prince's head,
    Which on the ground did fall
Still grumbling sore at Robin Hood
    To be so dealt withal.

The giants then began to rage
    To see their prince lie dead.
"Thou art the next," quoth Little John,
    "So guard thou well thy head."

His falchion then John whirled about;
    It was both keen and sharp.
He struck the giant to the belt
    And cut in twain his heart.

Will Scarlet well had played his part.
    The giant fell to his knee.
Quoth Will, "The devil can't break his fast
    Unless he have all three."

So with his falchion he ran him through,
    A deep and bloody wound.
The giant swore and foamed and cursed
    And then fell to the ground.

Now all the lists with cheers were filled.
    The skies they did resound.
This brought the Princess to herself,
    Who'd fallen in a swound.

The King and Queen and Princess fair
  Came walking to the place,
And gave the champions many thanks
  And did them further grace.

Then quoth the King, "Say whence you are
  That thus disguiséd came,
Whose valor speaks that noble blood
  Doth run through every vein."

"A boon! A boon!" quoth Robin Hood,
  "On my knees a boon I crave."
Then quoth the King, "Thy boon I grant.
  But ask, and thou shalt have."

"Then pardon I beg for my merry men
  Who are within the wood,
For Little John and Will Scarlet
  And for me, bold Robin Hood."

"Art thou Robin Hood?" then quoth the King.
  "For the valor you have shown,
Your pardons I do freely grant
  And welcome you each one.

"I promised the Princess as the prize.
  She can not wed all three."
"She shall choose," said Robin. Said Little John,
  "Then small share falls to me."

33

Then did the Princess view all three
 With a comely lovely grace.
She took Will Scarlet by the hand,
 Quoth, "Here I make my choice."

With that a noble lord stepped forth;
 Of Maxfield Earl was he.
He looked Will Scarlet in the face
 And wept most bitterly.

Quoth he, "I had a son like thee
 Whom I loved wondrous well.
But he is gone, or rather dead.
 His name was Young Gamwell."

Will Scarlet then fell to his knee;
 Cried, "Father, father! Here,
Here kneels your son, your Young Gamwell,
 You said you loved so dear."

O what embracing and kissing was there
 When all these friends were met!
They are gone to the wedding, and so to bedding,
 And so I bid you Good-night!

ROBIN HOOD AND THE CURTAL FRIAR

Merrily

1. In sum-mer time when leaves are green And flow-ers are fresh and gay, Rob-in Hood and his mer-ry men Were dis-posed to play.

2. "O, which of you can kill a buck? And who can kill a doe? Or who can kill a fine fat hart Five hun-dred feet him fro?"

3. Will Scar-let then he killed a buck; And Much he killed a doe; And Lit-tle John killed a fine fat hart Five hun-dred feet him fro.

36

"A blessing on thy heart," said Robin Hood,
    "That hath shot this shot for me.
I'd ride my horse an hundred miles
    To find a match for thee."

That caused Will Scarlet then to laugh;
    He laughed full heartily.
"In Fountains Abbey lives a friar
    Who can beat both him and thee.

That curtal friar in Fountains Dale
    Well can a strong bow draw.
He'll beat you and your yeomen all
    And set them in a row."

Robin took a solemn oath,
    It was by Mary free,
That he would neither eat nor drink
    Till the friar he did see.

Robin put on his harness good,
    On his head a cap of steel,
Broad sword and buckler by his side,
    And they became him well.

He took his bow into his hand,
    'Twas made of a trusty tree,
A sheaf of arrows at his belt;
    To the Fountains Dale went he.

And coming into Fountains Dale
    No further would he ride.
And there he saw a curtal friar
    Walking by the water-side.

The friar had on a harness good,
    On his head a cap of steel,
Broad sword and buckler by his side,
    And they became him well.

Robin lighted off his horse
    And tied him to a thorn.
"Carry me over the water, friar,
    Or else thy life's forlorn."

The friar took Robin on his back,
    Deep water he did bestride;
And spake word neither good nor bad
    Till he reached the other side.

Lightly leapt Robin from the friar's back.
    The friar said to him again,
"Carry me over this water, fellow,
    Or it shall cause thee pain."

Robin took the friar on his back;
    Deep water he did bestride;
And spake word neither good nor bad
    Till he came to the other side.

Lightly leapt the friar from Robin's back.
    Robin said to him again,
"Carry me over this water, friar,
    Or it shall cause thee pain."

The friar took Robin on his back again,
    Stepped in up to the knee.
Until he came to the middle stream
    Neither good nor bad spake he.

And coming to the middle stream,
    There he threw Robin in.
"Now, choose thee, choose thee, fine fellow,
    Whether thou wilt sink or swim."

Robin Hood swam to a bush of broom,
    The friar to a wicker wand.
Bold Robin Hood is gone to shore,
    And taken his bow in hand.

One of the arrows under his belt
    At the friar he let fly.
The curtal friar with his steel buckler
    He put that arrow by.

"Shoot on, shoot on, thou fine fellow,
    Shoot as thou hast begun.
If thou shoot all a summer's day
    Thy arrows I will not shun."

Robin Hood shot passing well
   Till his arrows all were gone.
They took their swords and steel bucklers
   And fought with might and main,

From ten o'clock that morning
   Till four in the afternoon.
Then Robin Hood came to his knees
   Of the friar to beg a boon.

A boon! A boon! thou curtal friar,
   I beg it on my knee.
Give me leave to set my horn to my mouth
   And to blow blasts three."

That will I do," the friar said,
   "Of thy blasts I have no doubt.
I hope thou wilt blow so passing well
   That both thine eyes fall out."

Robin Hood set his horn to his mouth;
   He blew but blasts three.
Fifty yeomen with good bows bent
   Came running o'er the lea.

A boon! A boon!" the friar said,
   "The like I gave to thee.
Give me leave to set my fist to my mouth
   And whistle whistles three."

That will I do," said Robin Hood,
   "Or else I were to blame.
Three whistles in a friar's fist
   Would make me glad and fain."

The friar set his fist to his mouth
   And whistled whistles three.
And half a hundred good ban-dogs
   Came running hastily.

Two dogs at once to Robin did go,
   One behind, the other before.
Robin's mantle of Lincoln green
   Off from his back they tore.

And whether his men shot east or west,
　Or they shot north or south,
The curtal dogs, as they were taught,
　Caught the arrows in their mouth.

"Take up thy dogs," said Little John,
　"Friar, at my bidding be."
"Whose man art thou," the friar said,
　"Comes here to prate with me?"

"I am Little John, Robin Hood's man;
　Friar, I do not lie.
If soon thou take not up thy dogs
　I'll take up them and thee."

Little John had a bow in his hand;
　He shot with might and main.
Soon half a score of the friar's dogs
　Lay dead upon the plain.

"Hold thy hand, good fellow," the friar said,
　"With thy master I'll agree.
And I shall take new orders now
　With all haste that may be."

"If thou'lt leave Fountains Dale," said Robin,
　"And Fountains Abbey free,
Every Sunday throughout all the year
　A noble shall be thy fee.

"And every holy day through the year,
　Changed shall thy garment be,
If thou wilt go to Nottingham
　And there remain with me."

The friar had lived in Fountains Dale
　Seven long years and more.
There was neither lord nor knight nor earl
　Could make him yield before.

ROBIN HOOD AND ALLEN A DALE

ROBIN HOOD AND ALLEN A DALE

Not too fast

1. Come, lis - ten to me, you gal - lants so free, All
2. As Rob - in Hood in the for - est stood All
3. The young - ster was clothed in scar - let red, In

you that love mirth for to hear, _____ And I will you tell of a
un - der the green - wood tree, _____ There was he a - ware of a
scar - let fine___ and gay, _____ And he___ did frisk it ___

bold ___ out - law That lived in Not - ting - ham - shire. _____
brave ___ young man As fine as fine ___ might be. _____
o - ver the plain ___ Chant - ing a roun - de - lay. _____

42

As Robin Hood next morning stood
  Amongst the leaves so gay,
He did espy the same young man
  Come drooping along the way.

The scarlet he wore the day before,
  It was clean cast away;
At every step he fetched a sigh,
  "Alack and welladay!"

Then stepped forth brave Little John
  And Much, the miller's son.
This made the young man bend his bow
  When as he saw them come.

"Stand off, stand off!" the young man said,
  "What is your will with me?"
"You must come before our master straight
  Under yon greenwood tree."

And when he came to Robin Hood,
  Robin asked courteously,
"O, hast thou any money to spare
  For my merry men and me?"

"I have no more," the young man said,
  "Than five shillings and a ring.
And that I have kept these seven long years
  To have at my wedding.

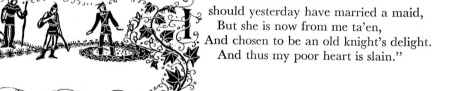
I should yesterday have married a maid,
But she is now from me ta'en,
And chosen to be an old knight's delight.
And thus my poor heart is slain."

"What is thy name?" then Robin Hood said,
"Come, say without any fail."
"By my troth," then said the young man,
"My name is Allen a Dale."

"What wilt thou give," said Robin Hood then,
"In ready gold or fee,
To help thee to thy true love again
And give her unto thee?"

"I have no money," quoth the young man,
"No ready gold nor fee.
But I will swear upon a book
Thy servant for to be."

"How many miles to thy true love?
Come, say without any guile."
"By my troth," then said the young man.
"It is but five little mile."

Then Robin Hood hastened over the plain,
He stayed not for anything,
Until he came unto the church
Where Allen should have his wedding.

"What dost thou here?" the Bishop said,
"I prithee now tell to me."
"A harper am I," said bold Robin Hood,
"The best in the North Countree."

"O welcome, O welcome," the Bishop cried,
"That music pleaseth me."
"Thou'lt have no music," said Robin Hood then,
"Till bride and bridegroom I see."

With that came in a wealthy knight
Who was both grave and old,
And after him a finikin lass
Who shone like glistering gold.

"This is no fit match," quoth bold Robin Hood,
"That you do seem to make here.
And since we are come unto the church
The bride shall choose her dear."

Then Robin put his horn to his mouth,
And blew blasts two or three;
And four and twenty bowmen bold
Came leaping over the lea.

And when they came into the church,
Marching in a row,
The very first man was Allen a Dale
To give bold Robin his bow.

"This is thy true love," then Robin said,
  "Young Allen, as I hear say.
And you shall be wed at this same time
  Before we go away."

"That shall not be," the Bishop said,
  "Thy word it shall not stand.
They shall be three times asked in the church,
  As is the law of our land."

Robin pulled off the Bishop's coat
  And put it on Little John.
"By my troth," then Robin Hood said,
  "This cloth doth make thee a man."

When Little John stepped into the choir,
  The folk began for to laugh.
He asked them seven times in the church,
  Lest three be not enough.

"Who gives me this maid?" then said Little John.
  Said Robin Hood, "That do I,
And he that doth take her from Allen a Dale,
  Full dearly he shall her buy."

Thus having ended this merry wedding,
  The bride looked fresh as a queen.
And so they returned to merry greenwood
  Amongst the leaves so green.

ROBIN HOOD AND MAID MARIAN

ROBIN HOOD AND MAID MARIAN

A bonny fine maid of a noble degree,
  Maid Marian called by name,
Did live in the North, of excellent worth,
  For she was a gallant dame.

T was neither Rosamond nor Jane Shore,
  Whose beauty was clear and bright,
That could surpass this country lass,
  Beloved of lord and knight.

The Earl of Huntington, nobly born,
  That came of noble blood,
To Marian went, with good intent,
  By the name of Robin Hood.

But fortune bore these lovers a spite,
  And soon they were forced to part.
To merry greenwood went Robin Hood
  With a sad and sorrowful heart.

And Marian, poor soul, was troubled in mind
　　For the absence of her friend.
With finger to eye, she'd often cry
　　And his person much commend.

Perplexed and vexed and troubled in mind,
　　She dressed herself like a page,
And searched the wood for Robin Hood,
　　The bravest of men in that age.

With quiver and bow, sword, buckler, and all,
　　Thus armed was Marian most bold,
Still wandering about to find Robin out,
　　Whose presence was better than gold.

But Robin Hood himself disguised,
　　And Marian was strangely attired.
So they proved foes, and fell to blows.
　　Her valor bold Robin admired.

They drew their swords and to cutting they went,
　　For at least an hour or more,
Till blood ran apace from Robin's face,
　　And Marian was wounded sore.

O hold thy hand," said Robin Hood,
    "And thou shalt be one of my string,
To range in the wood with bold Robin Hood,
    To hear the sweet nightingale sing."

W hen Marian heard her lover's voice,
    Her name she did confess.
With kisses sweet she did him greet,
    Like a most loyal lass.

W hen Robin Hood his Marian saw,
    O, what a hugging was there!
With kind embraces and kissing of faces,
    Providing of gallant cheer.

T hen Little John took his bow in his hand
    And wandered in the wood
To kill the deer and make good cheer
    For Marian and Robin Hood.

A stately banquet they had full soon,
    All in a shaded bower,
Where venison sweet they had to eat
    And were merry that present hour.

A t last they ended their merriment
    And went to walk in the wood,
Where Little John and Maid Marian
    Attended on Robin Hood.

ROBIN HOOD AND THE BISHOP

With much vigor

1. As it ___ fell out on a sun - shin - ing day When ___
2. And as ___ he walked a - long ___ the ___ wood, Some ___
3. "O, what shall I do?" said ___ Rob - in Hood ___ then, "If the

Phoe-bus was in ___ his ___ prime, Then ___ Rob - in ___ Hood, that
pas - time for ___ to ___ spy, There was he a - ware of a
Bis - hop doth ___ take me, No ___ mer - cy he'll show to

arch - er good, In mirth would spend some time.
Bis - hop proud And all his com - pa - ny.
me, I know, But hang - ed I shall be."

Then Robin was stout and turned him about.
And a little old house he did spy;
And to an old wife to save his life
He loud began to cry.

Why, who art thou?" said the old wife then,
"Come tell it me for good."
"I am an outlaw, as many do know;
My name is Robin Hood.

Yonder's the Bishop and all his men.
And if he doth take me,
Then day and night he'll work me spite,
And hangéd I shall be."

If thou be Robin," said the old wife,
"As thou dost seem to be,
For thee I'll provide, and thee I'll hide
From the Bishop's company.

For well I remember one Saturday night
Thou bought me shoes and hose.
Therefore I'll provide thyself to hide
And keep thee from thy foes."

Then give me soon thy coat of grey,
Take thou my mantle of green.
Thy spindle and twine to me resign,
Take thou my arrows keen."

When Robin Hood was thus arrayed,
    He went to his company.
With his spindle and twine, he looked behind
    For the Bishop's company.

O, who is yon?" said Little John,
    "That comes now over the lea?
An arrow will I at her let fly,
    So like a witch looks she."

O, hold thy hand," said Robin Hood,
    "Shoot not thy arrows keen.
I'm Robin Hood, thy master good,
    And soon it shall be seen."

The Bishop came to the old wife's house.
    He called in a furious mood,
"Come, let me soon see; bring unto me
    That traitor Robin Hood."

He set the old wife on a milk-white steed,
    Himself on a dapple-grey.
And for joy that he had caught Robin Hood
    He went laughing all the way.

54

But as they rode along the wood,
 The Bishop chanced to see
A hundred brave young bowmen bold
 Under the greenwood tree.

"**O**, who is yon?" the Bishop said,
 "That's ranging in the wood?"
"Marry," said the old wife, "I think it to be
 A man called Robin Hood."

"**T**hen who art thou," the Bishop said,
 "Whom I have here with me?"
"Why, I'm an old wife, Sir Bishop," she said,
 "Look closely, and you shall see."

"**T**hen woe is me," the Bishop said,
 "That ever I saw this day!"
He turned him about, but Robin stout
 Called him and bade him stay.

Then Robin took hold of the Bishop's horse
 And tied him fast to a tree.
And Little John smiled his master upon,
 For joy of that company.

Robin took his cloak from his back
    And spread it on the ground,
And out of the Bishop's portmanteau
    He told five hundred pound.

Now let him go," said Robin Hood,
    Said John, "That may not be.
I vow and protest he shall sing us a mass
    Before he go from me."

Then Robin took the Bishop by the hand
    And bound him fast to a tree,
And made the Bishop sing a mass
    For him and his yeomanry.

And then they brought him through the wood
    And set him on his dapple-grey,
And gave him the tail within his hand,
    And bade him for Robin pray.

ROBIN HOOD AND THE BUTCHER

With energy and marked rhythm

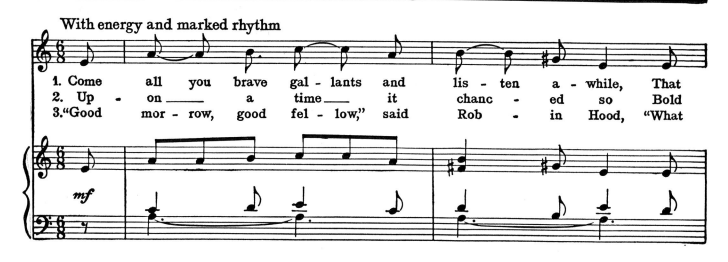

1. Come all you brave gal - lants and lis - ten a - while, That
2. Up - on a time it chanc - ed so Bold
3. "Good mor - row, good fel - low," said Rob - in Hood, "What

are in these bow - ers with - in, Of Rob - in Hood, that
Rob - in in for - est spied A butch - er with a
food hast thou? Tell un - to me. Thy trade to me tell, and

ar - cher good, A song I in - tend for to sing.
bon - ny fine mare Who to the mar - ket hied.
where thou dost dwell, For I like well thy com - pa - ny."

The butcher he answered Robin Hood,
"No matter where I dwell.
A butcher I am, and to Nottingham
I'm going, my flesh to sell."

"What is the price of thy flesh?" said Robin,
"Come, tell it soon unto me,
The price of thy mare, be she never so dear,
For a butcher I fain would be."

"The price of my flesh," the butcher replied,
"I soon will tell to thee.
With my bonny mare, and they are not dear,
Four marks thou must give to me."

"Four marks I will give thee," said Robin Hood,
"Four marks it shall be thy fee.
Thy money come count, and let me mount,
For a butcher I fain would be."

Now Robin Hood is to Nottingham gone
To enter the butcher's trade.
With good intent to the Sheriff he went
And there his stand he made.

When other butchers opened their meat,
Bold Robin he then begun.
But how for to sell he knew not well,
For a butcher he was but young.

When other butchers no meat could sell,
    Robin got gold and fee;
For he sold more for one penny
    Than others could sell for three.

And when he sold his meat so fast,
    No butcher near him could thrive;
For he sold more for one penny
    Than others could sell for five.

This made the butchers of Nottingham
    To wonder as they did stand.
"Surely he is some prodigal
    That hath sold his father's land."

The butchers stepped to jolly Robin
    Acquainted with him to be.
"Come, brother," one said, "we be all of one trade.
    Come, will you go dine with me?"

Accurst be his heart," said Robin Hood,
    "That a butcher doth deny.
I'll go with you, my brethren true,
    As fast as I can hie."

But when to the Sheriff's house they came
    To dinner they hied apace.
And Robin he the man must be
    Before them to say grace.

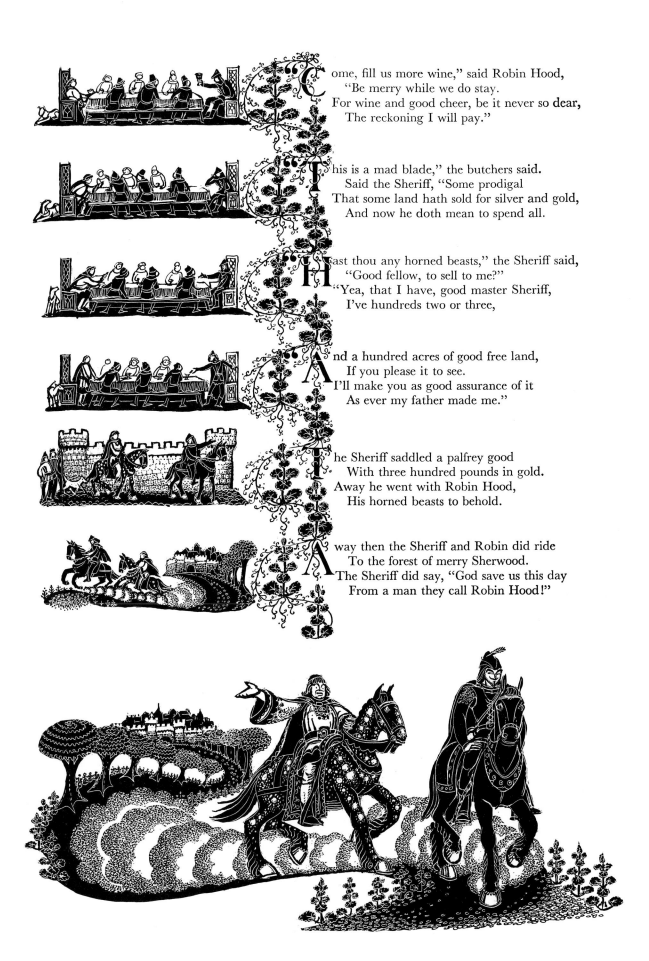

"Come, fill us more wine," said Robin Hood,
  "Be merry while we do stay.
For wine and good cheer, be it never so dear,
  The reckoning I will pay."

"This is a mad blade," the butchers said.
  Said the Sheriff, "Some prodigal
That some land hath sold for silver and gold,
  And now he doth mean to spend all.

"Hast thou any horned beasts," the Sheriff said,
  "Good fellow, to sell to me?"
"Yea, that I have, good master Sheriff,
  I've hundreds two or three,

"And a hundred acres of good free land,
  If you please it to see.
I'll make you as good assurance of it
  As ever my father made me."

The Sheriff saddled a palfrey good
  With three hundred pounds in gold.
Away he went with Robin Hood,
  His horned beasts to behold.

Away then the Sheriff and Robin did ride
  To the forest of merry Sherwood.
The Sheriff did say, "God save us this day
  From a man they call Robin Hood!"

But when a little further they came,
  Bold Robin Hood chanced to spy
A hundred head of good red deer
  Come tripping the Sheriff nigh.

How like you my horned beasts, master Sheriff?
  They're fat and fair to see."
"I tell thee, good fellow, I would I were gone,
  For I like not thy company."

Then Robin he set his horn to his mouth
  And blew but blasts three.
And quickly anon there came Little John
  And all his company.

What is your will?" then said Little John,
  "Good master, come tell it me."
"I've brought the Sheriff of Nottingham
  This day to dine with me."

He is welcome to me," then said Little John,
  "I hope he will honestly pay.
I know he has gold, if it be but well told,
  Will serve us for drink a whole day."

Then Robin took his cloak from his back
  And spread it upon the ground,
And out of the Sheriff's portmanteau
  He told three hundred pound.

Then Robin he brought him through the wood
  And set him on his dapple-grey.
"Commend me to your wife at home!"
  So Robin went laughing away.

ROBIN HOOD AND THE BOLD PEDLAR

ROBIN HOOD AND THE BOLD PEDLAR

With much vigor

1. There chanced to be a ped - lar bold, A
2. By chance he met two stub - born blades, Two
3. "O ped - lar, what is in thy pack? Come

ped - lar bold he chanced to be; He rolled his pack all
stub - born blades they chanced to be; The one of them was
spee - di - ly and tell to me." "I've sev - 'ral suits of

on his back, And he came trip - ping
Rob - in Hood, The oth - er was Lit - tle
gay green silk, And sil - ken bow - strings

o'er the lea.
John so free.
two or three."

Down down a down, down down a down.

"If you've sev'ral suits of the gay green silk
And silken bow-strings two or three,
Then by my faith," said Little John,
"Half your pack shall belong to me."

"O nay, O nay," said the pedlar bold,
"O nay, that can never be.
There's never a man in Nottingham
Can take half my pack from me."

Then the pedlar he pulled off his pack
And put it down below his knee.
"If you move me one perch from this,
Pack and all shall go with thee."

Then Little John he drew his sword,
The pedlar by his pack did stand;
They fought until they both did sweat.
John cried, "Pedlar, hold your hand!"

Robin Hood was standing by,
And he did laugh most heartily,
"I could find a man of a smaller scale
Could thrash the pedlar and also thee."

Then Robin Hood he drew his sword,
The pedlar by his pack did stand.
They fought till the blood in streams did flow.
Robin cried, "Pedlar, hold your hand.

"O, pedlar, pedlar, what is thy name?
Come speedily and tell to me."
"My name, my name I ne'er will tell
Till your names you have told to me."

The one of us is Robin Hood,
The other Little John so free."
"Now," said the pedlar, "'Tis my will
Whether my name I tell to thee.

I am Gamble Gold of the gay green woods
And traveled far beyond the sea.
For killing a man in my father's land
From my home I am forced to flee."

If you're Gamble Gold of the gay green woods
And traveled far beyond the sea,
You are my mother's sister's son.
What nearer cousins can we be?"

They sheathed their swords with friendly words,
So merrily they did agree.
They went to an inn and there they dined,
And bottles cracked most merrily.

ROBIN HOOD AND GUY OF GISBORNE

Thus said Robin Hood to Little John
    In greenwood where they lay,
"I dreamt of two wight yeomen
    Who set on me this day.

"I thought they did me beat and bind
    And took from me my bow.
If I be Robin alive in this land
    I'll be quit with both them two."

"Dreams are swift, master," said Little John,
    "As the wind that blows over the hill.
For if it be never so loud this night,
    Tomorrow it may be still."

"Busk ye, bown ye, my merry men all,
    For John shall go with me;
For I'll go seek yon wight yeomen
    In greenwood where they be."

They put on their gowns of green;
    A-shooting gone are they,
Until they met a wight yeoman,
    His body against a tree.

A sword and a dagger he wore at his side,
    They'd been many a man's bane;
And he was clad in his horse's hide,
    Top and tail and mane.

"Stand you still, master," quoth Little John,
    "Under this trusty tree,
And I'll go to yon wight yeoman
    To learn what he may be."

"Ah, John, by me thou sets no store,
    And that's a bitter thing.
How oft send I my men before
    And stay myself behind?

"It is no cunning a knave to know,
  If a man but hear him speak.
And were it not for bursting my bow,
  Thy head, John, would I break."

But often words may foster harm.
    Thus parted Robin and John.
John has gone to Barnesdale
    Whose paths he knows each one.

And when he came to Barnesdale,
    Great sorrow there he had.
He found that two of his fellows
    Were slain both in a glade.

Scarlet a-foot was flying
    Over stock and stone.
For the Sheriff with seven score men
    Fast after him was gone.

John bent up a good yew bow
    And bent it back to shoot.
The bow was made of a tender bough
    And fell down at his foot.

"Woe worth thee, wicked wood," said John,
    "That e'er thou grew on tree!
This day thou art my sorrow
    My boon when thou shouldst be."

And it is said, when men be met,
    Six can do more than three.
And they have taken Little John
    And bound him to a tree.

Let us leave talking of Little John,
    For he is bound to a tree,
And talk of Guy and Robin Hood
    In greenwood where they be.

69

Good morrow, good fellow," quoth Sir Guy,
"Good morrow, good fellow," quoth he,
"Methinks by this bow thou bears in thy hand
A good archer thou must be.

I have lost my way," then quoth Sir Guy,
"All in the morning tide."
"I'll lead thee through the wood," said Robin,
"Good fellow, I'll be thy guide."

I seek an outlaw," quoth Sir Guy,
"Men call him Robin Hood.
I had rather meet him on a day
Than forty pounds of gold."

Let us some pastime make," said Robin,
"Let us walk in the wood,
And when we do not look for him,
We may meet with Robin Hood."

They cut them down the summer wands
Which grew beneath a briar,
And set them three score rods apart
To shoot the arrows near.

Lead on, good fellow," said Sir Guy,
"Lead on, I do bid thee."
"Nay, by my faith," quoth Robin Hood,
"The leader thou shalt be."

The first good shot that Robin shot,
Not an inch the prick shot fro;
Guy was an archer good enough,
But he could ne'er shoot so.

A blessing on thy heart," said Guy,
"Thy shooting is full good.
If thy heart be as good as thy hands
Thou wert better than Robin Hood.

Tell me thy name, good fellow," said Guy,
"Under the leaves of lyne."
"Nay, by my faith," said Robin Hood,
"Till thou have told me thine."

I dwell by dale and down," quoth Guy,
"And I've done many a cursed turn.
And he that calls me my right name
Calls me Guy of good Gisborne."

"My dwelling is in the wood," said Robin,
"By thee I set right naught.
I am Robin Hood of Barnesdale,
A fellow thou long hast sought."

He that had been neither kith nor kin
Might have seen a full fair sight,
To see how together these yeomen went
With blades both brown and bright,

To see how together these yeomen fought
    Two hours of a summer's day.
'Twas neither Guy nor Robin Hood
    That thought to fly away.

Robin tripped upon a root
    And stumbled at that tide.
And Guy was quick and nimble withal
    And hit him o'er the side.

Robin thought upon Our Lady dear
    And soon leapt up again.
And thus he came with a back-hand stroke,
    And good Sir Guy has slain.

He said, "Lie there, O good Sir Guy,
    And with me be not wroth.
If thou'st had the worse strokes at my hand,
    Thou shalt have the better cloth."

Then Robin doffed his gown of green;
    On Guy he did it throw,
And he put on that horse's hide
    That clad him from top to toe.

The bow, the arrows, the little horn,
    All with me now I'll bear;
For now I'll go to Barnesdale
    To see how my men do fare."

obin set Guy's horn to his mouth,
A loud blast he did blow.
This heard the Sheriff of Nottingham
Where he lay under a low.

"Hearken! Hearken!" said the Sheriff,
"I hear tidings good.
Yonder I hear Sir Guy's horn blow;
He hath slain Robin Hood.

"Yonder I hear Sir Guy's horn blow,
It blows so well in tide.
And yonder comes that wight yeoman
Clad in his horse's hide.

"Come hither, O thou good Sir Guy,
Ask of me what thou'lt have."
"I'll none of thy gold," said Robin Hood,
"Nor I'll none of it have.

"But now the master I have slain," he said,
"Let me go strike the knave.
This is the whole reward I ask,
Nor other will I have."

"Thou art a madman," said the Sheriff,
A knight's fee thou shouldst have had.
Well granted shall thy asking be
Since it hath been so bad."

Then Robin went to Little John
  To loose his bonds anon.
The Sheriff and his company
  Fast after him have gone.

"Stand back! Stand back!" said Robin Hood,
  "Why draw you me so near?
'Twas never the custom in our country
  One's shrift another should hear."

Robin pulled forth an Irish knife
  And loosed John hand and foot.
He gave him Guy's bow in his hand
  And bade it be his boot.

Then John took Guy's bow in his hand, —
  His arrows were tipped with blood; —
The Sheriff saw John draw his bow
  To shoot there where he stood.

Then to his house in Nottingham
  He fled full fast away;
And so did all his company.
  Not one behind did stay.

ROBIN HOOD AND THE GOLDEN ARROW

With much expression

mf

1. Once when the sher-iff of Not-ting-ham Was pla-gued sore with grief, He talked no good of Rob-in Hood, That strong and stur-dy thief.

2. So to the Lon-don road he passed, His loss-es to un-fold Un to the King, who lis-tened to The tale the sher-iff told.

3. "Why," quoth the King, "what shall I do? Art thou not sher-iff for me? Go, take thy course. The law en-force On them that in-jure thee!"

G o, get thee gone, and by thyself
   Make up some tricking game
For to enthrall the rebels all.
   Go, take thy course with them."

S o then the Sheriff he returned,
   And on the way he thought,
Of the words of the King, and how the thing
   To pass might well be brought.

W ith that he hit upon a plan,
   A shooting-match to hold;
And he that shot the best of all
   Should have a prize of gold.

A n arrow with a golden head
   And shaft of silver white,
Who won the day should bear away
   For his own proper right.

F or in his mind the Sheriff thought
   That when such matches were,
Those outlaws stout, beyond all doubt,
   Would be the bowmen there.

T idings came to Robin Hood
   Under the greenwood tree.
"Prepare you then, my merry men,
   We'll go yon sport to see."

W ith that stepped forth a brave young man,
   David of Doncaster.
"Master," said he, "be warned by me.
   From greenwood do not stir.

T o tell the truth, I'm well informed
   Yon match is but a wile.
The Sheriff, I wiss, is planning this
   Us archers to beguile."

Thou speaks like a coward," said Robin Hood,
  "Thy words do not please me.
Come what will, I'll try my skill
  At yon brave archery."

Then bespoke brave Little John,
  "Come, let us thither go.
Come, listen to me, how it shall be
  That the Sheriff need not know.

Our mantles all of Lincoln green
  Behind us we shall leave.
We'll dress us all so differently
  They shall not us perceive.

One shall wear white, another red,
  One yellow, another blue.
Thus in disguise to the exercise
  We'll go, whate'er ensue."

Forth from the greenwood they are gone
  With hearts all firm and stout,
And mixed them with the Sheriff's men
  To have a hearty bout.

The Sheriff looking round about
  Among eight hundred men,
He could not see the sight that he
  Had long expected then.

Some said, "If Robin Hood were here,
  And all his men to boot,
Sure none of them could pass these men,
  So bravely do they shoot."

"Ay," quoth the Sheriff, and scratched his head,
  "I thought he would be here.
I thought he would, but, though he's bold,
  He dare not now appear."

That word struck Robin to the heart.
    It rankled in his blood.
"E'er long," thought he, "Thou well shalt see
    That here was Robin Hood."

Some cried, "Blue jacket!" Another, "Brown!"
    The third cried, "Brave yellow!"
The fourth man said, "Yon man in red
    In this place has no fellow."

For that was Robin Hood himself,
    For he was clothed in red.
At every shot the prize he got;
    His aim was sure and dead.

The arrow with the golden head
    And shaft of silver white
Brave Robin won, and bore with him
    For his own proper right.

The outlaws then that very day,
    To shun all kind of doubt,
By three or four, no less, no more,
    As they went in, came out,

Until they all were met again
    Under the greenwood shade,
Where they report in pleasant sport
    What brave pastime they made.

Said Robin Hood, "My only care
    Is how yon Sheriff may
Know certainly that it was I
    Who bore his prize away."

Said Little John, "My counsel good
    Did take effect before.
So therefore now, if you'll allow,
    I will advise once more."

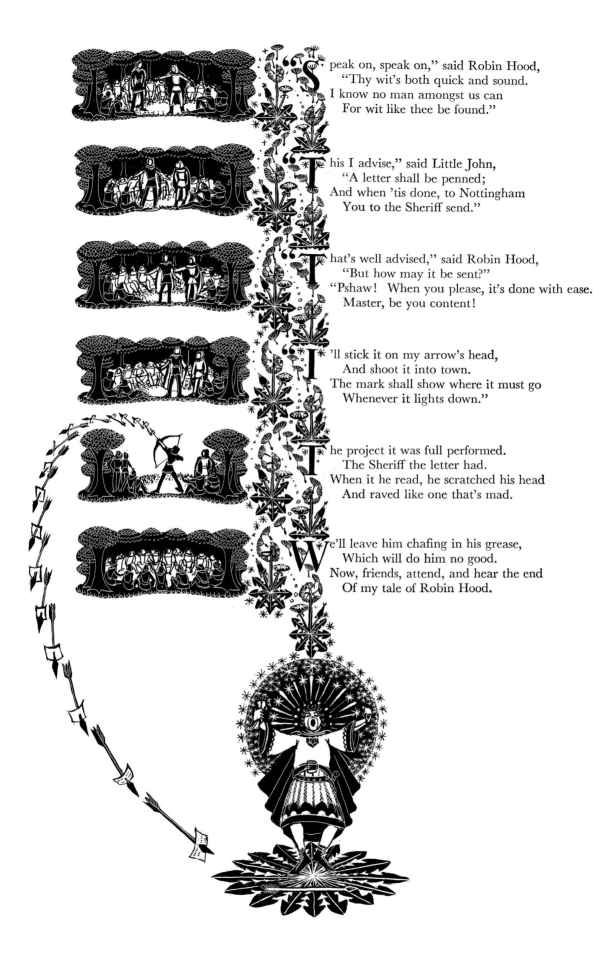

"Speak on, speak on," said Robin Hood,
  "Thy wit's both quick and sound.
I know no man amongst us can
  For wit like thee be found."

"This I advise," said Little John,
  "A letter shall be penned;
And when 'tis done, to Nottingham
  You to the Sheriff send."

"That's well advised," said Robin Hood,
  "But how may it be sent?"
"Pshaw! When you please, it's done with ease.
  Master, be you content!

"I'll stick it on my arrow's head,
  And shoot it into town.
The mark shall show where it must go
  Whenever it lights down."

The project it was full performed.
  The Sheriff the letter had.
When it he read, he scratched his head
  And raved like one that's mad.

We'll leave him chafing in his grease,
  Which will do him no good.
Now, friends, attend, and hear the end
  Of my tale of Robin Hood.

ROBIN HOOD AND THE RANGER

ROBIN HOOD AND THE RANGER

Gaily, with marked rhythm

non legato

1. When Phoe - bus had melt - ed the sick - les of ice And like - wise the moun - tains of snow, _____ Bold Rob - in Hood he would

2. He left all his mer - ry men wait - ing be - hind, As through the green val - leys he passed. _____ There did he be - hold a

3. "I'm go - ing," said Rob - in, "To kill a fat buck For me and my mer - ry men all; _____ Be - sides, e'er I go, I'll

ram - ble   to   see,   To __ frol - ic   a - broad with his   bow. _____
for - es - ter   bold,   Who __ cried out, "Friend, whith - er   so   fast?" _____
have   a   fat   doe,   Or __ else   it   shall   cost   me   a   fall." _____

"Y ou'd best have a care," said the forester then,
    "For these are His Majesty's deer.
Before you shall shoot, the thing I'll dispute,
    For I am head forester here."

"T hese thirteen long summers," quoth Robin, "I'm sure,
    My arrows I here have let fly
Where freely I range. Methinks it is strange
    You should have more power than I.

"T his forest," quoth Robin, "I think is my own,
    And so are the nimble deer, too.
Therefore I declare and solemnly swear
    I will not be thwarted by you."

T he forester he had a long quarter-staff,
    Likewise a broad sword by his side.
Without more ado, he presently drew,
    Declaring the truth should be tried.

B old Robin Hood had a sword of the best;
    Thus, ere he would take any wrong,
His courage was bright, he'd venture a fight,
    And thus they fell to it, ding dong.

T he very first blow that the forester gave,
    He made his broad weapon cry, "Twang!"
'Twas o'er Robin's head. He fell down for dead.
    O, that was a terrible bang!

But Robin Hood soon did recover himself,
    And bravely fell to it again.
The very next stroke, their weapons were broke,
    Yet never a man there was slain.

At quarter-staff they then resolvéd to play,
    Because they would have t'other bout.
And brave Robin Hood right valiantly stood,
    Unwilling was he to give out.

At length in a rage the bold forester flew
    And cudgeled bold Robin so sore
That he could not stand; so, shaking his hand,
    He said, "Let us freely give o'er.

Thou art a brave fellow; I needs must confess
    I never knew any so good.
Thou'rt fitting to be a yeoman for me
    And range in the merry greenwood.

'll give thee this ring as a token of love,
    For bravely thou acted thy part.
That man that can fight, in him I delight
    And love him with all my whole heart."

hen Robin Hood, setting his horn to his mouth,
    A blast there he merrily blows.
His yeomen did hear, and straight did appear
    A hundred with trusty long-bows.

ow Little John came at the head of them all,
    Clothed in a rich mantle of green.
And likewise the rest were gloriously dressed,
    A beautiful sight to be seen.

o, these are my yeomen," said Robin Hood then,
    "And thou shalt be one of the train.
A quiver and a bow, a mantle also
    I give them whom I entertain."

he forester willingly entered the list;
  They were such a beautiful sight.
Then with a long-bow they shot a fat doe
  And made a rich supper that night.

obin Hood gave him a mantle of green,
  Broad arrows, a curious long-bow.
This done, the next day, so gallant and gay,
  He gathered them all in a row.

uoth he, "My brave yeomen, be true to your trust,
  And then we may range the woods wide."
They all did declare and solemnly swear
  They'd conquer, or die by his side.

ROBIN HOOD RESCUING WILL STUTLY

With much feeling and expression

1. When Rob - in Hood in the green - wood lived, Un -
3. When Rob - in Hood he ____ heard this news, O
5. He clothed him - self in ____ scar - let then; His

der the green - wood tree, Ti - - dings there came, to
he was griev - ed sore. Aye, and so to his brave
men were all in green. A ____ fin - er show through-

him with speed, Ti - dings for cer - tain - ty, 2. That
men he spoke, Who al - to - geth - er swore 4. That
out the world In no place could be seen. 6. Forth

Will Stut - ly sur - pri - sed was, And eke in pris - on
Will Stut - ly should res - cued be And brought home safe a -
from the green - wood they are gone, Yea, all cour - age - ous -

lay; Three var - lets that the
gain; Or else should man - y a
ly, Re - solv - ing to bring

rit.

f

sher - iff hired Did base - ly him be - tray.
gal - lant wight For his sake there be slain.
Stut - ly home Or ev - 'ry man to die.

p quietly

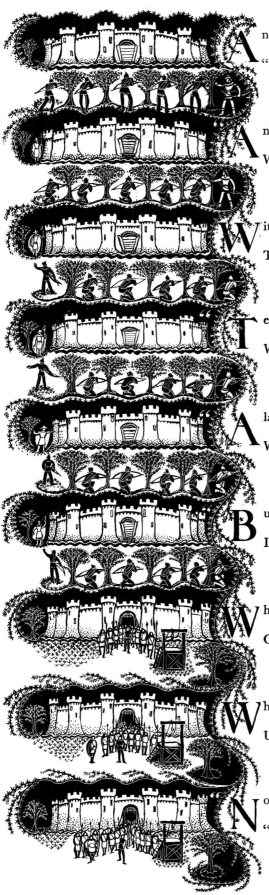

And when they came the castle near
  In which Will Stutly lay,
"I think it good," said Robin Hood,
  "We here in ambush stay,

And send one forth some news to hear
  Of yonder palmer fair,
Who stands under the castle wall.
  Some news he may declare."

With that stepped forth a brave young man
  Who was of courage bold.
Thus he did say to the old man,
  "I pray thee, palmer old,

Tell me, if thou dost rightly know,
  When must Will Stutly die,
Who's one of bold Robin's men
  And here doth prisoner lie?"

Alack! Alas!" the palmer said,
  "Forever woe is me!
Will Stutly must be hanged this day
  On yonder gallows tree."

But fare thou well, thou good old man,
  Farewell, and thanks to thee.
If Stutly hangéd be this day
  Avenged his death shall be."

When he was from the palmer come,
  The gates were opened wide.
Out of the castle Stutly came,
  Guarded on every side.

When he was forth from the castle come,
  And saw no help was nigh,
Unto the Sheriff he did say,
  Thus he said gallantly,

Now, seeing that I needs must die,
  Grant me one boon," said he,
"My noble master ne'er had man
  That yet was hanged on tree.

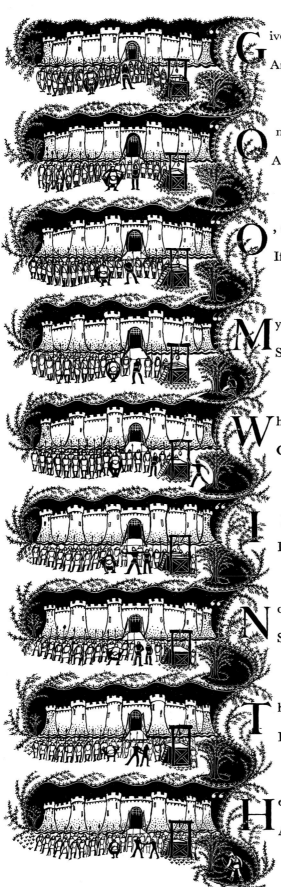

"Give me a sword all in my hand
    And let me be unbound,
And with thee and thy men I'll fight
    Till I lie dead on ground."

"O no! O no!" the Sheriff said,
    "On gallows thou shalt die!
Aye, and so shall die thy master too,
    If e'er in me it lie."

"O, dastard coward," Stutly cried,
    "Faint-hearted peasant slave!
If ever my master do thee meet,
    Thy payment thou shalt have.

"My noble master doth thee scorn,
    And all thy cowardly crew.
Such silly imps unable are
    Bold Robin to subdue!"

When Stutly was to the gallows come,
    And thought to bid adieu,
Out of a bush leapt Little John
    And stepped Will Stutly to.

"I pray thee, Will, before thou die,
    Of thy dear friends take leave.
I needs must borrow him awhile.
    How say you, Master Shreeve?"

"Now, as I live," the Sheriff said,
    "That varlet will I know.
Some sturdy outlaw is this man.
    Therefore let him not go."

Then Little John so hastily
    Away cut Stutly's bands;
From one of the proud Sheriff's men
    A sword twitched from his hands.

"Here, Stutly, here! Take thou this sword;
    Thou canst it better sway.
And here defend thyself a while,
    For aid will come straightway."

And there they turned them back to back
　In the middle of the fray,
Till Robin Hood approachéd near
　With many an archer gay.

At that an arrow by them flew,
　I wist from Robin Hood.
"Make haste, make haste," the Sheriff said,
　"Make haste, for haste is good."

The Sheriff fled; his sturdy men
　Thought it not good to stay;
But as their master had them taught
　They ran full fast away.

"O stay, O stay!" Will Stutly cried,
　"Take leave e'er you retreat;
You ne'er will catch bold Robin Hood
　Unless you dare him meet.

A little thought when I came here,
　When I came to this place,
That I would meet with Little John
　Or see my master's face."

Thus Stutly was released again
　And safe brought from his foe.
"O thanks, O thanks to my master dear,
　Since here it was not so.

And once again, my fellows all,
　In greenwood we shall meet,
Where we shall make our bow-strings **twang**
　For us their music sweet."

ROBIN HOOD AND THE BISHOP OF HEREFORD

Pompously

1. Some they will talk of bold Rob - in Hood, And
2. As it be - fell in mer - ry Barnes - dale, All
3. Said Rob - in, "Come, kill a ve - ni - son, Come,

some of bar - ons bold. But I'll tell you of the Bish - op of
un - der the green - wood tree, The Bish - op of He - re - ford
kill me a good fat deer. The Bish - op of He - re - ford

He - re - ford, When they robbed him of his gold.
was to come by With all his com - pa - ny.
shall dine with me And pay well for his cheer."

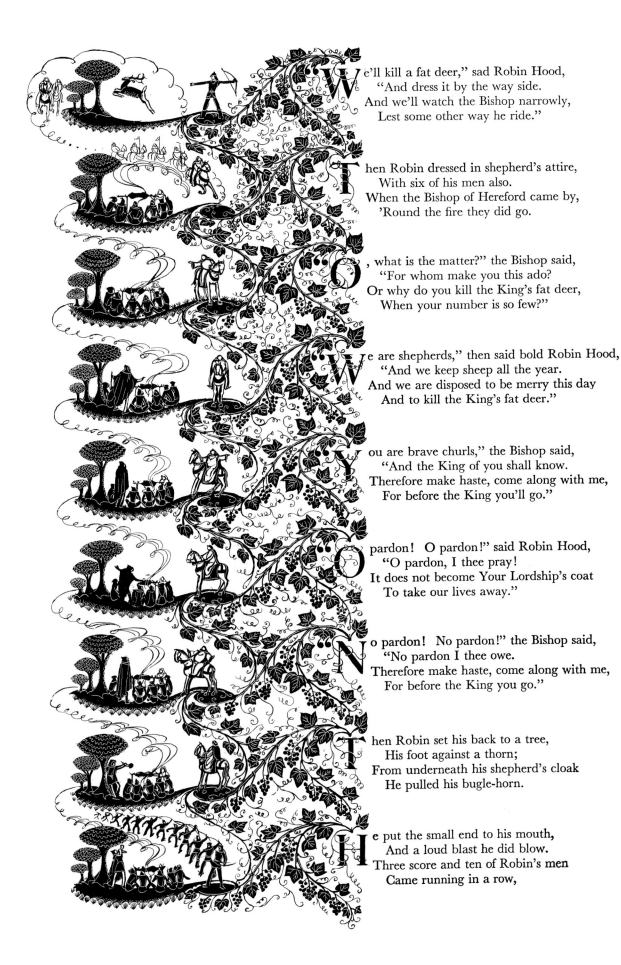

"We'll kill a fat deer," sad Robin Hood,
 "And dress it by the way side.
And we'll watch the Bishop narrowly,
 Lest some other way he ride."

Then Robin dressed in shepherd's attire,
 With six of his men also.
When the Bishop of Hereford came by,
 'Round the fire they did go.

"O, what is the matter?" the Bishop said,
 "For whom make you this ado?
Or why do you kill the King's fat deer,
 When your number is so few?"

"We are shepherds," then said bold Robin Hood,
 "And we keep sheep all the year.
And we are disposed to be merry this day
 And to kill the King's fat deer."

"You are brave churls," the Bishop said,
 "And the King of you shall know.
Therefore make haste, come along with me,
 For before the King you'll go."

"O pardon! O pardon!" said Robin Hood,
 "O pardon, I thee pray!
It does not become Your Lordship's coat
 To take our lives away."

"No pardon! No pardon!" the Bishop said,
 "No pardon I thee owe.
Therefore make haste, come along with me,
 For before the King you go."

Then Robin set his back to a tree,
 His foot against a thorn;
From underneath his shepherd's cloak
 He pulled his bugle-horn.

He put the small end to his mouth,
 And a loud blast he did blow.
Three score and ten of Robin's men
 Came running in a row,

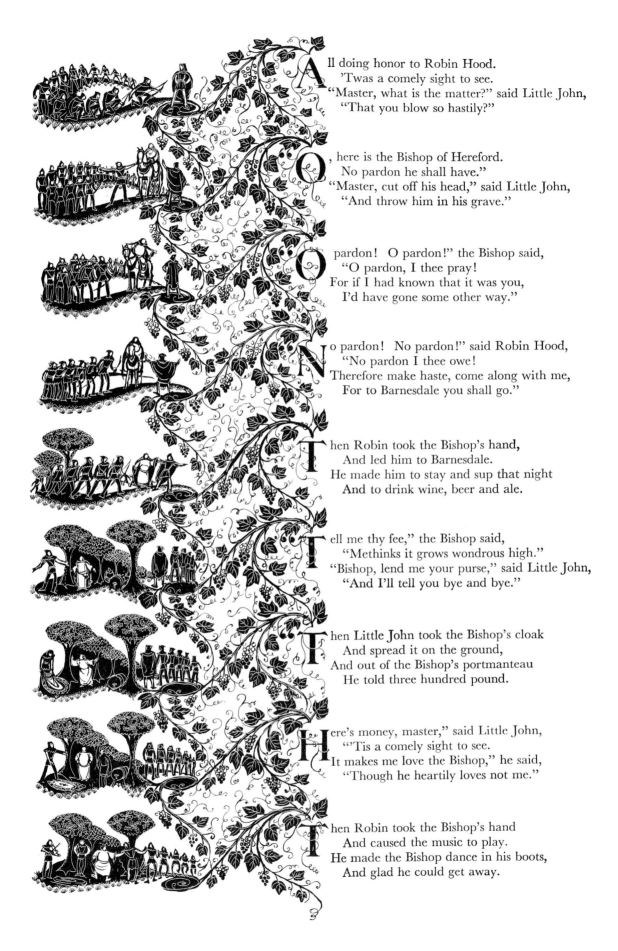

All doing honor to Robin Hood.
  'Twas a comely sight to see.
"Master, what is the matter?" said Little John,
  "That you blow so hastily?"

O, here is the Bishop of Hereford.
  No pardon he shall have."
"Master, cut off his head," said Little John,
  "And throw him in his grave."

O pardon! O pardon!" the Bishop said,
  "O pardon, I thee pray!
For if I had known that it was you,
  I'd have gone some other way."

No pardon! No pardon!" said Robin Hood,
  "No pardon I thee owe!
Therefore make haste, come along with me,
  For to Barnesdale you shall go."

Then Robin took the Bishop's hand,
  And led him to Barnesdale.
He made him to stay and sup that night
  And to drink wine, beer and ale.

Tell me thy fee," the Bishop said,
  "Methinks it grows wondrous high."
"Bishop, lend me your purse," said Little John,
  "And I'll tell you bye and bye."

Then Little John took the Bishop's cloak
  And spread it on the ground,
And out of the Bishop's portmanteau
  He told three hundred pound.

Here's money, master," said Little John,
  "'Tis a comely sight to see.
It makes me love the Bishop," he said,
  "Though he heartily loves not me."

Then Robin took the Bishop's hand
  And caused the music to play.
He made the Bishop dance in his boots,
  And glad he could get away.

ROBIN HOOD'S GOLDEN PRIZE

ROBIN HOOD'S GOLDEN PRIZE

With energy and humor

1. I____ have heard talk of bold Rob - in Hood, And____
2. But____ such a tale as____ this be - fore I____
3. Like____ to a fri - ar bold Rob - in Hood Was____

of brave Lit - tle John, Of Fri - ar Tuck and____
think was nev - er none. For Rob - in Hood dis -
dressed in his ar - ray. With hood, gown, beads, and____

Will Scar - let, Of____ Locks - ley and Maid Mar - i - an.
guised him - self And____ to____ the____ wood has gone.
cru - ci - fix He____ walked a - long the way.

He had not gone miles two or three
 When he did chance to spy
Two lusty priests clad all in black
 Come riding gallantly.

"*Benedicite!*" then said Robin Hood,
 "Some pity on me take.
Cross you my hand with a silver groat
 For Our dear Lady's sake.

I have been wandering all this day
 And nothing could I get,
Not so much as one cup of drink
 Nor bit of bread to eat."

"Now, by my faith," the priests replied,
 "We never a penny have;
For we this morning have been robbed,
 And could no money save."

"I am much afraid," said Robin Hood,
 "You both do tell a lie.
And now before that you go hence,
 Your word I mean to try."

When this the priests heard Robin say,
 They rode away amain;
But Robin betook him to his heels
 And soon met them again.

hen Robin Hood laid hold of them
   And pulled them from their horse.
"O, spare us, friar!" the priests cried out,
   "On us have some remorse!"

"ou said you had no gold," quoth he,
   "Wherefore, without delay,
We three will fall down on our knees.
   For money we will pray."

he priests they could not him refuse,
   But down they knelt with speed.
"Send us, O, send us," then quoth they,
   "Some money to serve our need."

hen they'd been praying an hour's space,
   The priests did still lament.
Then quoth bold Robin, "Now let's see
   What heaven hath us sent.

100

"We will be sharers all alike
    Of the money that we have.
And there is never a one of us
    His fellows shall deceive."

The priests their hands in their pockets put,
    But gold they could find none.
"We'll search ourselves," said Robin Hood,
    "Each other, one by one."

Robin took pains to search them both.
    He found good store of gold.
Five hundred pieces presently
    Upon the grass were told.

"Here's a brave show," said Robin Hood,
    "Such store of gold to see;
And you shall each one have a part,
    For you prayed so heartily."

He gave them fifty pounds apiece;
    The rest himself did keep.
The priests they dared not speak one word,
    But they sighed wondrous deep.

With that the priests rose from their knees,
    Thinking they would leave him so.
"Nay, stay," said Robin, "One thing more
    I'll say before you go.

"You shall be sworn," said Robin Hood,
    "Upon this holy grass,
That you will never tell lies again,
    Which way soe'er you pass.

"The other oath you shall take is this:
    Have charity for the poor.
Say you have met with a holy friar,
    And I desire no more."

He set them on their horses then;
    Away then they did ride.
To merry greenwood he returned
    With great joy, mirth, and pride.

ROBIN HOOD RESCUING THREE SQUIRES

ROBIN HOOD RESCUING THREE SQUIRES

Lively

1. There are___ twelve months___ in
2. Now Rob - in Hood is to
3. "What news?___ What news,___ thou

all___ the year, As I___ hear man - y men
Not - ting - ham gone, With a link a down and a
sil - ly old woman? What news___ hast thou___ for

say; _____ But the mer - ri - est month___ in
day, _____ And there he met a sil - ly
me?" _____ Said___ she, _____ "Three squires___ in

104

all — the year Is the mer - ry month of May. ———
old — wom - an Who was weep - ing on the way. ———
Not - ting - ham town To - day are con - demned to die." ———

"O, have they parishes burnt?" he said,
    "Or have they ministers slain?
Or have they robbed any virgin maid,
    Or other men's wives have ta'en?"

They have no parishes burnt, good sir,
    Nor yet have ministers slain,
Nor have they robbed any virgin maid,
    Nor other men's wives have ta'en."

"O, what have they done?" said bold Robin Hood.
    "I pray thee tell to me."
"They've slain the king's own fallow deer
    And born their long-bows with thee."

Now Robin Hood is to Nottingham gone,
    With a link a down and a day,
And there he met a silly old palmer
    Who was walking along the way.

What news? What news, thou silly old man?
    What news, I do thee pray?"
Said he, "Three squires in Nottingham town
    Are condemned to die this day."

Come, change thy apparel with me, old man,
    Come, change thy apparel with mine.
Here's forty shillings in silver good;
    Go drink it in beer or wine."

"O thine apparel is good," he said,
    "And mine is ragged and torn.
Wherever you go, wherever you ride,
    Laugh not an old man to scorn."

"Come, change thy apparel with me, old churl,
    Come, change thy apparel with mine.
Here's twenty pieces of good broad gold;
    Go, feast thy brethren with wine."

Robin put on the old man's hat.
    It stood full high on the crown.
He said, "The first bargain that I come at,
    It shall make thee come down."

Then he put on the old man's cloak.
    'Twas patched black, blue, and red.
He thought it no shame the whole day long
    To wear the bags of bread.

Then he put on the old man's breeks,
    Were patched from front to side.
"By the truth of my body," bold Robin did say,
    "This man had little pride."

Then he put on the old man's hose,
    Were patched from knee to wrist.
"By the truth of my body," said bold Robin Hood,
    "I'd laugh if I had any list."

Then he put on the old man's shoes,
  Were patched beneath and aboon.
Then Robin Hood swore a solemn oath,
  "It's clothing that makes a man!"

Now Robin Hood is to Nottingham gone,
  With a link a down and a down.
And there he met with the Sheriff proud,
  Who was walking along the town.

O save, O save, O Sheriff!" he said,
  "O save, and you may see!
And what will you give to a silly old man
  Who would your hangman be?"

Some suits, some suits," the Sheriff he said,
  "Some suits I'll give to thee;
Some suits, some suits, and pence thirteen
  Today are a hangman's fee."

Then Robin he turned him round about
  And jumped from stock to stone.
"By the truth of my body," the Sheriff said,
  "Well jumped, thou nimble old man."

I ne'er was a hangman in all my life,
  Nor yet will I enter the trade;
But curst be he," said Robin Hood,
  "That first a hangman was made.

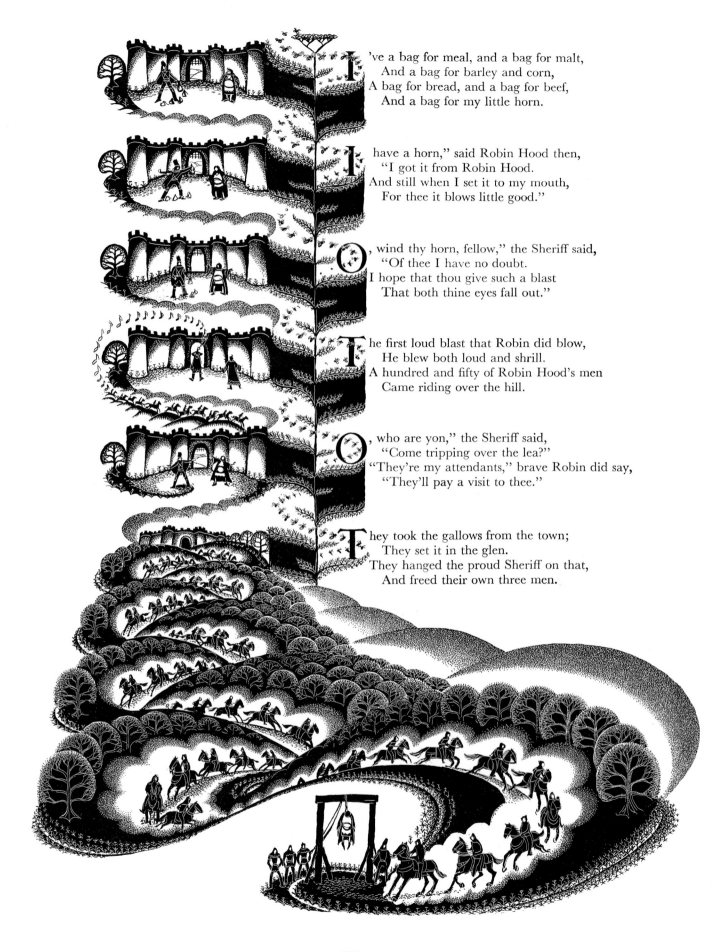

I've a bag for meal, and a bag for malt,
  And a bag for barley and corn,
A bag for bread, and a bag for beef,
  And a bag for my little horn.

I have a horn," said Robin Hood then,
  "I got it from Robin Hood.
And still when I set it to my mouth,
  For thee it blows little good."

O, wind thy horn, fellow," the Sheriff said,
  "Of thee I have no doubt.
I hope that thou give such a blast
  That both thine eyes fall out."

The first loud blast that Robin did blow,
  He blew both loud and shrill.
A hundred and fifty of Robin Hood's men
  Came riding over the hill.

O, who are yon," the Sheriff said,
  "Come tripping over the lea?"
"They're my attendants," brave Robin did say,
  "They'll pay a visit to thee."

They took the gallows from the town;
  They set it in the glen.
They hanged the proud Sheriff on that,
  And freed their own three men.

ROBIN HOOD'S DEATH

ROBIN HOOD'S DEATH

Slowly, mournfully

p

like tolling bells

1. When Rob - in Hood and Lit - tle John Went
3. "O, do not go," Will Scar - let said, "Mas -
5. "The Prior - ess is my aunt's daugh - ter And

o'er yon bank of broom, Said Rob - in Hood to
ter, be warned by me, Un - less half a hun - dred of
nigh un - to my kin. She'll do me no harm," said

Lit - tle John, We have shot for man - y a pound. 2. Now
your best men You take___ to go with thee?" 4. "For
Rob - in Hood, "For all___ the world to win?" 6. Now

And when he came to Kirkly Hall,
　　He knocked upon the pin.
None was so ready as the Prioress
　　To let bold Robin in.

Will you sit down," the Prioress said,
　　"And drink some beer with me?"
"No, I will never eat nor drink
　　Till I am blooded by thee."

I have a room," the Prioress said,
　　"Which you did never see,
And if you please to walk therein,
　　You shall be blooded by me."

She blooded him in a vein of the arm
　　And locked him up in the room.
Then did he bleed all the live-long day
　　Until the next day at noon.

And first it bled the thick, thick blood;
　　And afterward the thin.
And then good Robin Hood knew well
　　Treason there was within.

He thought him of a window there,
　　Thinking he would get down.
But he was so weak he could not leap,
　　He could not get him down.

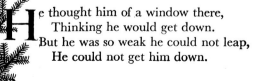

He thought him of his bugle-horn
  Which hung down at his knee.
He set his horn unto his mouth
  And blew out weak blasts three.

Then Little John, when hearing him
  As he sat under a tree,
"I fear my master is now near dead,
  He blows so wearily."

Little John is to Kirkly gone
  As fast as he can hie.
And when he came to Kirkly Hall
  He broke locks two or three,

Until he came to bold Robin Hood.
  Then he fell on his knee.
"A boon! A boon!" cried Little John,
  "Master, I beg of thee!"

"What is that boon," said Robin Hood,
  "John, that thou beg of me?"
"It is to burn fair Kirkly Hall
  And all their nunnery."

"Now nay, now nay!" quoth Robin Hood,
  "That boon I'll not grant thee.
I never hurt woman in all my time,
  Nor at mine end shall it be.

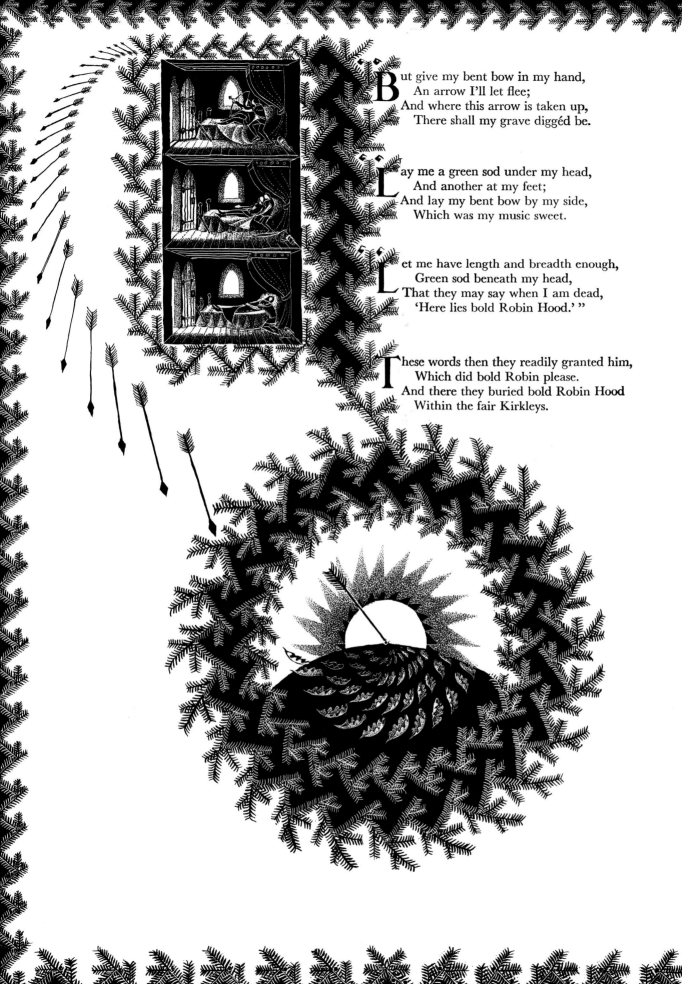

But give my bent bow in my hand,
    An arrow I'll let flee;
And where this arrow is taken up,
    There shall my grave diggéd be.

Lay me a green sod under my head,
    And another at my feet;
And lay my bent bow by my side,
    Which was my music sweet.

Let me have length and breadth enough,
    Green sod beneath my head,
That they may say when I am dead,
    'Here lies bold Robin Hood.' "

These words then they readily granted him,
    Which did bold Robin please.
And there they buried bold Robin Hood
    Within the fair Kirkleys.

THE END

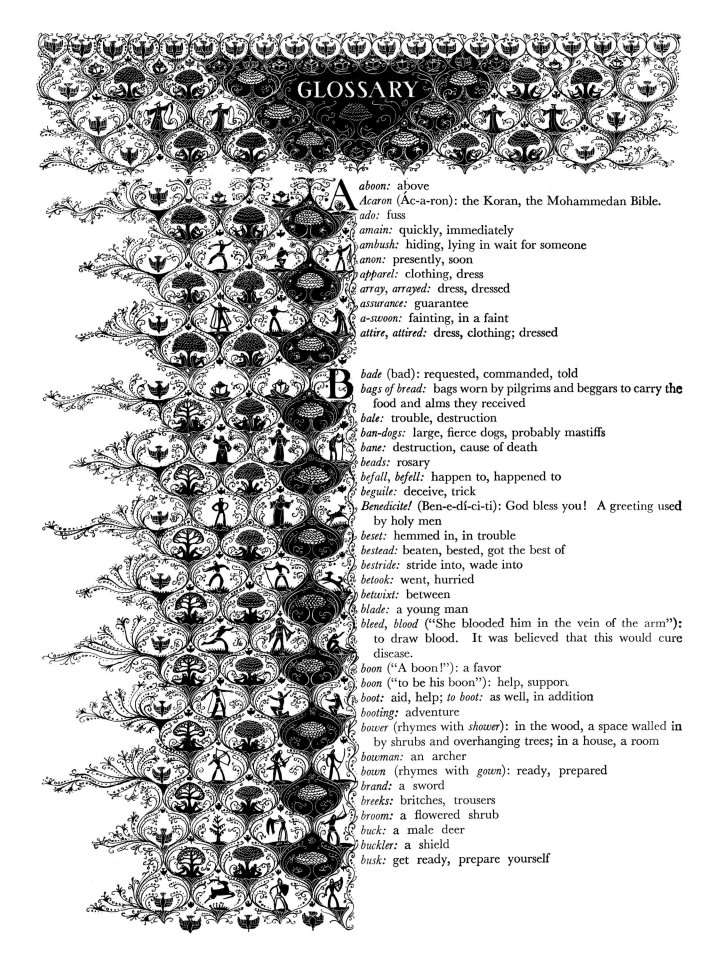

GLOSSARY

A

aboon: above

Acaron (Ác-a-ron): the Koran, the Mohammedan Bible.

ado: fuss

amain: quickly, immediately

ambush: hiding, lying in wait for someone

anon: presently, soon

apparel: clothing, dress

array, arrayed: dress, dressed

assurance: guarantee

a-swoon: fainting, in a faint

attire, attired: dress, clothing; dressed

B

bade (bad): requested, commanded, told

bags of bread: bags worn by pilgrims and beggars to carry the food and alms they received

bale: trouble, destruction

ban-dogs: large, fierce dogs, probably mastiffs

bane: destruction, cause of death

beads: rosary

befall, befell: happen to, happened to

beguile: deceive, trick

Benedicite! (Ben-e-dí-ci-ti): God bless you! A greeting used by holy men

beset: hemmed in, in trouble

bestead: beaten, bested, got the best of

bestride: stride into, wade into

betook: went, hurried

betwixt: between

blade: a young man

bleed, blood ("She blooded him in the vein of the arm"): to draw blood. It was believed that this would cure disease.

boon ("A boon!"): a favor

boon ("to be his boon"): help, support

boot: aid, help; *to boot:* as well, in addition

booting: adventure

bower (rhymes with *shower*): in the wood, a space walled in by shrubs and overhanging trees; in a house, a room

bowman: an archer

bown (rhymes with *gown*): ready, prepared

brand: a sword

breeks: britches, trousers

broom: a flowered shrub

buck: a male deer

buckler: a shield

busk: get ready, prepare yourself

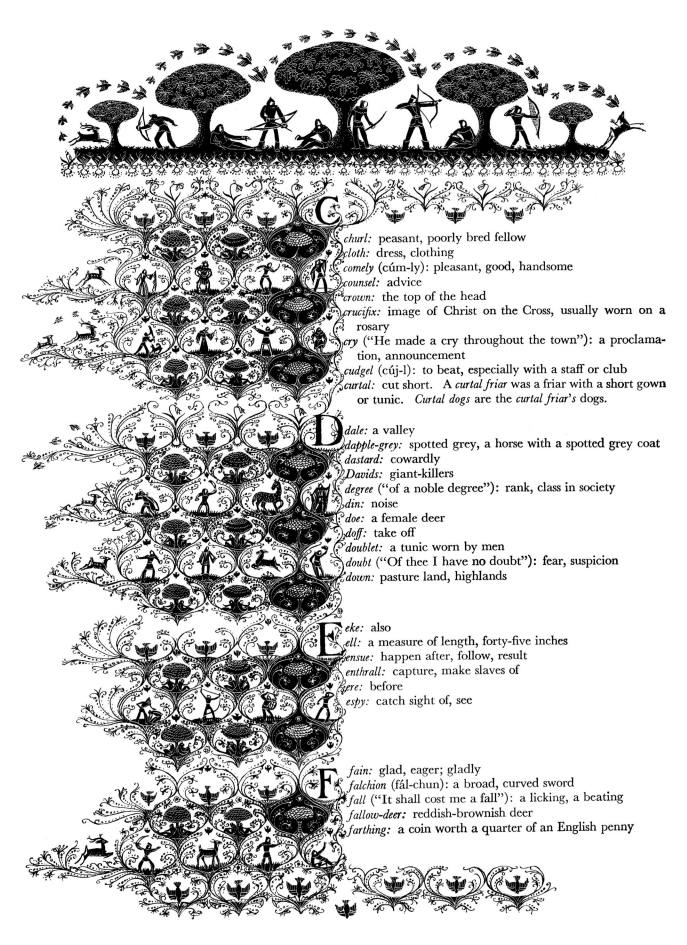

C

churl: peasant, poorly bred fellow

cloth: dress, clothing

comely (cúm-ly): pleasant, good, handsome

counsel: advice

crown: the top of the head

crucifix: image of Christ on the Cross, usually worn on a rosary

cry ("He made a cry throughout the town"): a proclamation, announcement

cudgel (cúj-l): to beat, especially with a staff or club

curtal: cut short. A *curtal friar* was a friar with a short gown or tunic. *Curtal dogs* are the *curtal friar's* dogs.

D

dale: a valley

dapple-grey: spotted grey, a horse with a spotted grey coat

dastard: cowardly

Davids: giant-killers

degree ("of a noble degree"): rank, class in society

din: noise

doe: a female deer

doff: take off

doublet: a tunic worn by men

doubt ("Of thee I have no doubt"): fear, suspicion

down: pasture land, highlands

E

eke: also

ell: a measure of length, forty-five inches

ensue: happen after, follow, result

enthrall: capture, make slaves of

ere: before

espy: catch sight of, see

F

fain: glad, eager; gladly

falchion (fál-chun): a broad, curved sword

fall ("It shall cost me a fall"): a licking, a beating

fallow-deer: reddish-brownish deer

farthing: a coin worth a quarter of an English penny

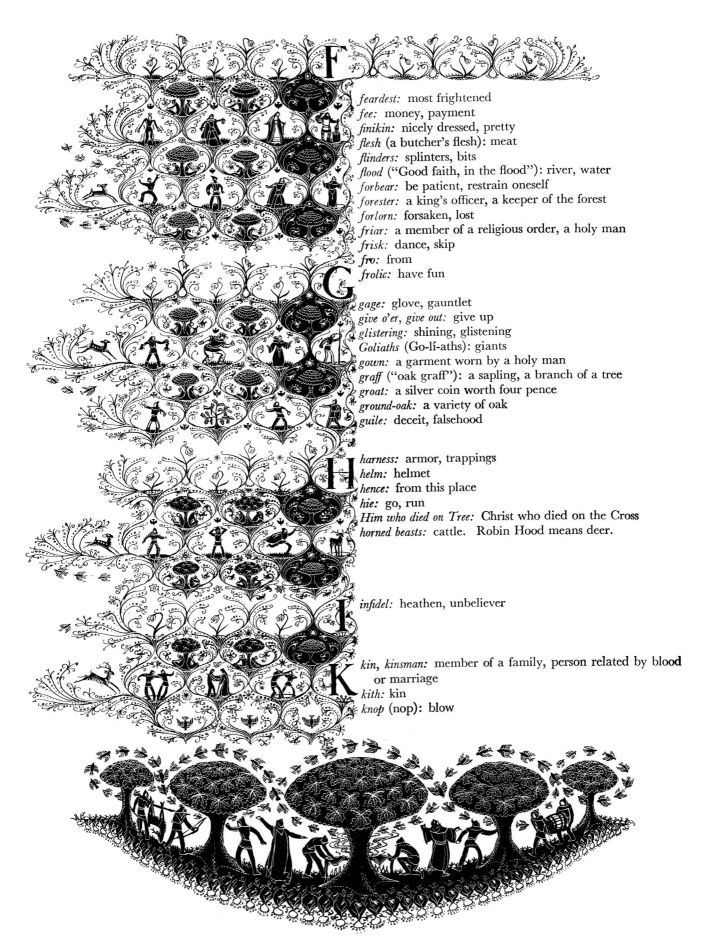

F

feardest: most frightened
fee: money, payment
finikin: nicely dressed, pretty
flesh (a butcher's flesh): meat
flinders: splinters, bits
flood ("Good faith, in the flood"): river, water
forbear: be patient, restrain oneself
forester: a king's officer, a keeper of the forest
forlorn: forsaken, lost
friar: a member of a religious order, a holy man
frisk: dance, skip
fro: from
frolic: have fun

G

gage: glove, gauntlet
give o'er, give out: give up
glistering: shining, glistening
Goliaths (Go-lí-aths): giants
gown: a garment worn by a holy man
graff ("oak graff"): a sapling, a branch of a tree
groat: a silver coin worth four pence
ground-oak: a variety of oak
guile: deceit, falsehood

H

harness: armor, trappings
helm: helmet
hence: from this place
hie: go, run
Him who died on Tree: Christ who died on the Cross
horned beasts: cattle. Robin Hood means deer.

I

infidel: heathen, unbeliever

K

kin, kinsman: member of a family, person related by blood
    or marriage
kith: kin
knop (nop): blow

119

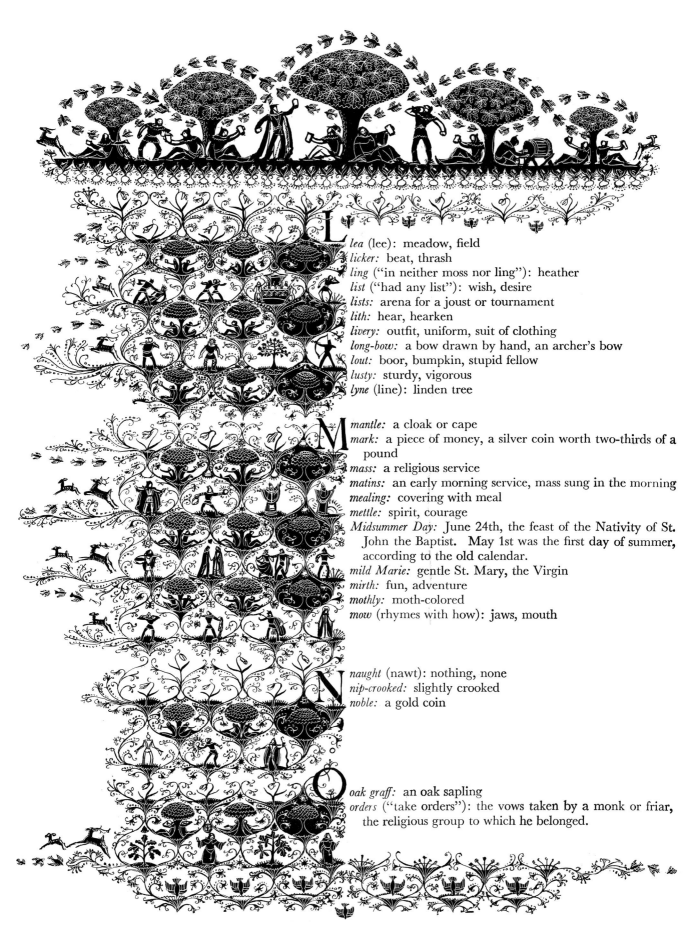

lea (lee): meadow, field
licker: beat, thrash
ling ("in neither moss nor ling"): heather
list ("had any list"): wish, desire
lists: arena for a joust or tournament
lith: hear, hearken
livery: outfit, uniform, suit of clothing
long-bow: a bow drawn by hand, an archer's bow
lout: boor, bumpkin, stupid fellow
lusty: sturdy, vigorous
lyne (line): linden tree

mantle: a cloak or cape
mark: a piece of money, a silver coin worth two-thirds of a
   pound
mass: a religious service
matins: an early morning service, mass sung in the morning
mealing: covering with meal
mettle: spirit, courage
Midsummer Day: June 24th, the feast of the Nativity of St.
   John the Baptist. May 1st was the first day of summer,
   according to the old calendar.
mild Marie: gentle St. Mary, the Virgin
mirth: fun, adventure
mothly: moth-colored
mow (rhymes with how): jaws, mouth

naught (nawt): nothing, none
nip-crooked: slightly crooked
noble: a gold coin

oak graff: an oak sapling
orders ("take orders"): the vows taken by a monk or friar,
   the religious group to which he belonged.

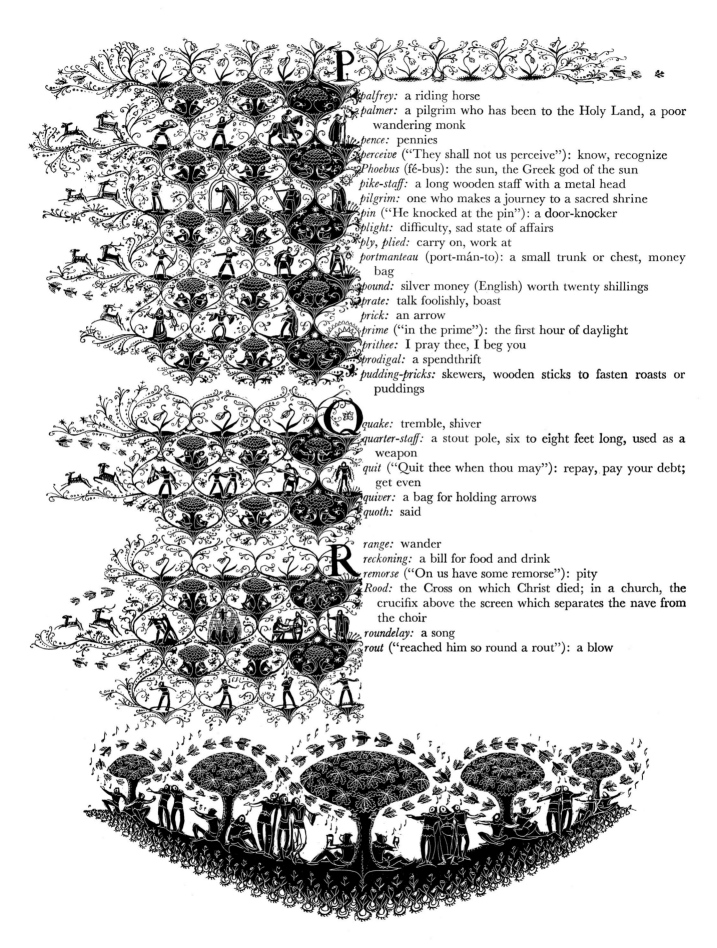

P

palfrey: a riding horse

palmer: a pilgrim who has been to the Holy Land, a poor wandering monk

pence: pennies

perceive ("They shall not us perceive"): know, recognize

Phoebus (fé-bus): the sun, the Greek god of the sun

pike-staff: a long wooden staff with a metal head

pilgrim: one who makes a journey to a sacred shrine

pin ("He knocked at the pin"): a door-knocker

plight: difficulty, sad state of affairs

ply, plied: carry on, work at

portmanteau (port-mán-to): a small trunk or chest, money bag

pound: silver money (English) worth twenty shillings

prate: talk foolishly, boast

prick: an arrow

prime ("in the prime"): the first hour of daylight

prithee: I pray thee, I beg you

prodigal: a spendthrift

pudding-pricks: skewers, wooden sticks to fasten roasts or puddings

Q

quake: tremble, shiver

quarter-staff: a stout pole, six to eight feet long, used as a weapon

quit ("Quit thee when thou may"): repay, pay your debt; get even

quiver: a bag for holding arrows

quoth: said

R

range: wander

reckoning: a bill for food and drink

remorse ("On us have some remorse"): pity

Rood: the Cross on which Christ died; in a church, the crucifix above the screen which separates the nave from the choir

roundelay: a song

rout ("reached him so round a rout"): a blow

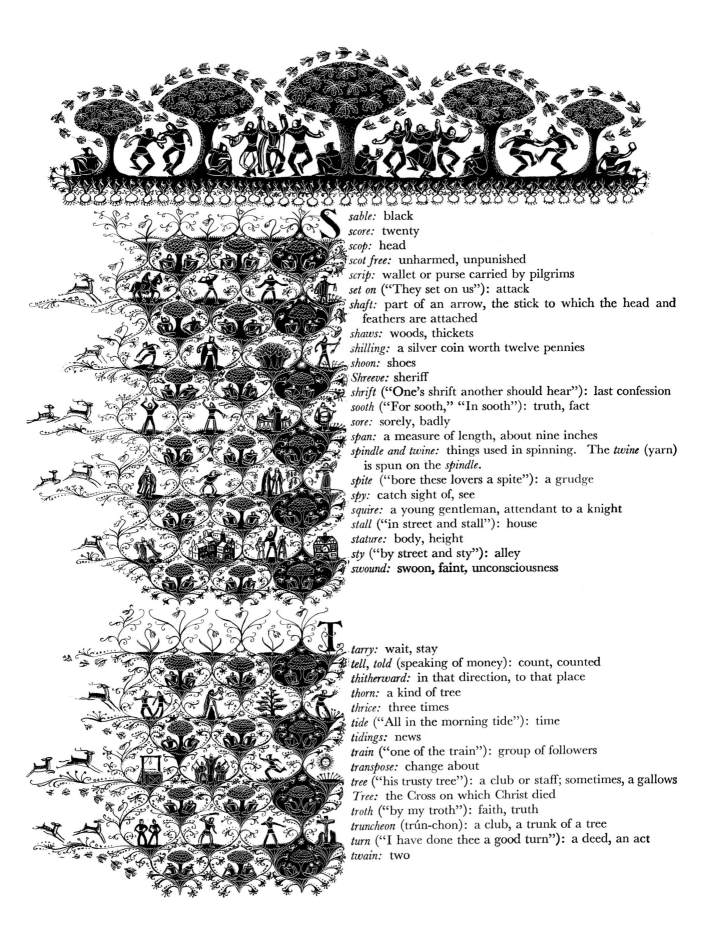

sable: black

score: twenty

scop: head

scot free: unharmed, unpunished

scrip: wallet or purse carried by pilgrims

set on ("They set on us"): attack

shaft: part of an arrow, the stick to which the head and feathers are attached

shaws: woods, thickets

shilling: a silver coin worth twelve pennies

shoon: shoes

Shreeve: sheriff

shrift ("One's shrift another should hear"): last confession

sooth ("For sooth," "In sooth"): truth, fact

sore: sorely, badly

span: a measure of length, about nine inches

spindle and twine: things used in spinning. The *twine* (yarn) is spun on the *spindle*.

spite ("bore these lovers a spite"): a grudge

spy: catch sight of, see

squire: a young gentleman, attendant to a knight

stall ("in street and stall"): house

stature: body, height

sty ("by street and sty"): alley

swound: **swoon, faint, unconsciousness**

tarry: wait, stay

tell, told (speaking of money): count, counted

thitherward: in that direction, to that place

thorn: a kind of tree

thrice: three times

tide ("All in the morning tide"): time

tidings: news

train ("one of the train"): group of followers

transpose: change about

tree ("his trusty tree"): a club or staff; sometimes, a gallows

Tree: the Cross on which Christ died

troth ("by my troth"): faith, truth

truncheon (trún-chon): a club, a trunk of a tree

turn ("I have done thee a good turn"): a deed, an act

twain: two

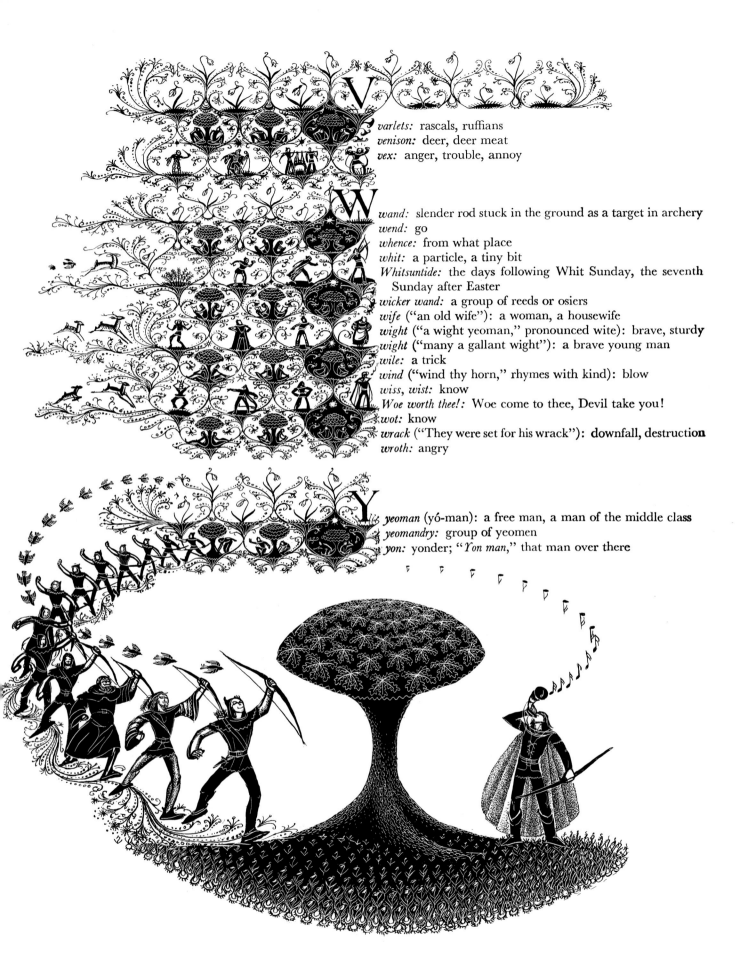

varlets: rascals, ruffians
venison: deer, deer meat
vex: anger, trouble, annoy

wand: slender rod stuck in the ground **as a target in archery**
wend: go
whence: from what place
whit: a particle, a tiny bit
Whitsuntide: the days following Whit Sunday, the seventh
    Sunday after Easter
wicker wand: a group of reeds or osiers
wife ("an old wife"): a woman, a housewife
wight ("a wight yeoman," pronounced wite): brave, sturdy
wight ("many a gallant wight"): a brave young man
wile: a trick
wind ("wind thy horn," rhymes with kind): blow
wiss, wist: know
Woe worth thee!: Woe come to thee, Devil take you!
wot: know
wrack ("They were set for his wrack"): **downfall, destruction**
wroth: angry

yeoman (yó-man): a free man, a man of the middle class
yeomandry: group of yeomen
yon: yonder; "*Yon man,*" that man over there

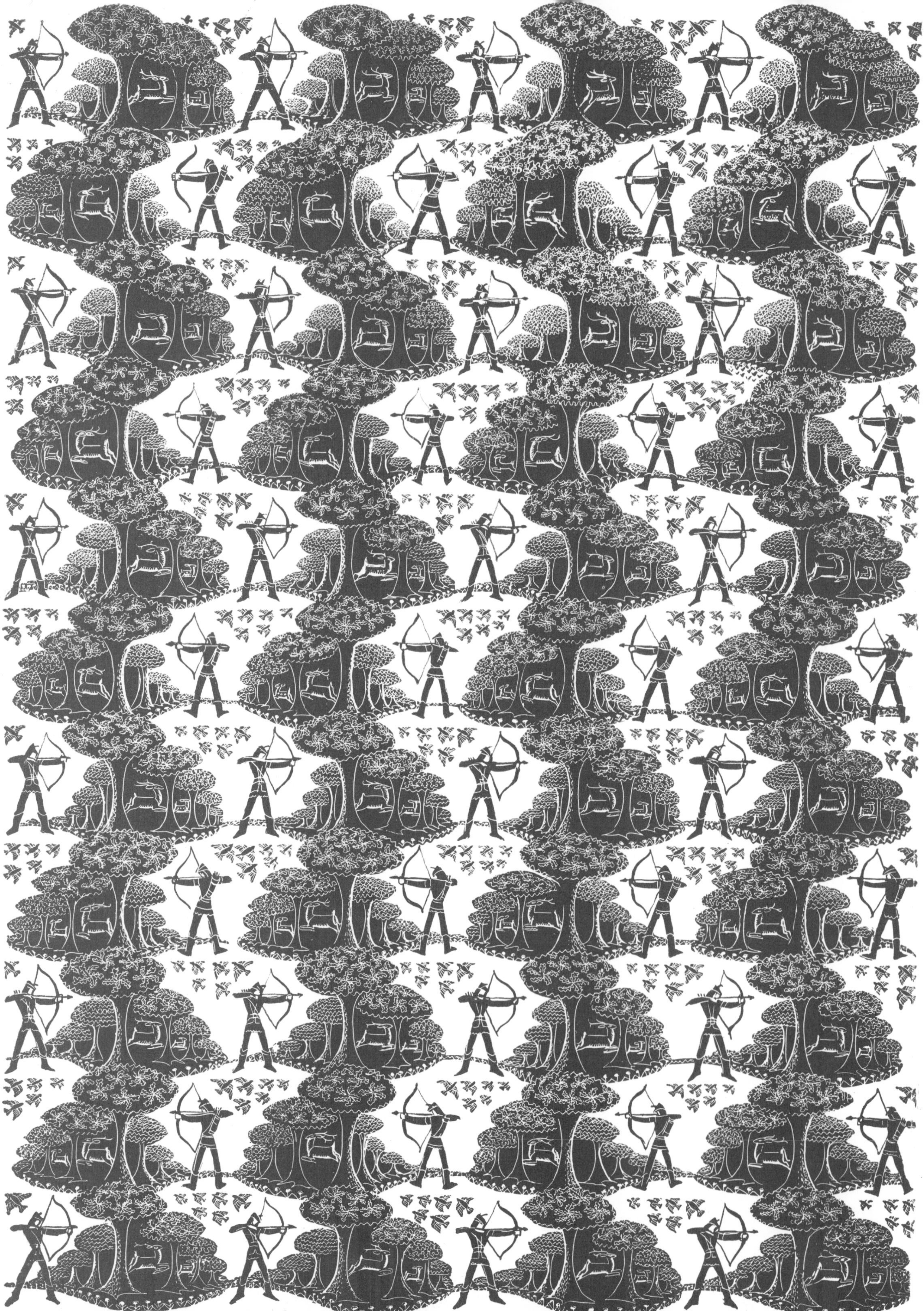